MW00413383

# VERA'S GENERATION

MIAH CROSBY

# CHAPTER ONE

Humans were a long-gone memory of the Hooni's evolutionary past. They filled history books and lended themselves to children's stories. Few Hooni gave much attention to the archaic people, even though the human's demise shaped the Hooni civilization.

Shortly before the humans inevitably wiped themselves out of existence a group of a few hundred locked themselves into a safe zone, cut off from the rest of the world. With a smaller gene pool, and isolated geographical location it inevitably produced physical changes in the humans living there. So much so that there came a point over many thousands of years where they were left with no alternative but to declare themselves a new species. Hooni was the name that Homo sapiens 2.0 adopted. Their appearance was similar to ancient humans but much smaller. The tallest among them was rarely above four feet tall. They also sported larger eyes and ears than the previous model had. Everyone had a creamy Sun-kissed tan color to their skin and their fingers had become a half-length longer. They were a strikingly beautiful people. It was reminiscent of the fairy like people from human mythology.

They live on what was once Borneo. The land had come up for sale during the early stages of the last global human conflicts. The countries that owned the large island were desperate for money to fund weapons and get food for their militant civilians. The world had become radicalized, every day was a fight to survive. If famine, plagues, and their neighbors didn't kill them the governments would be sure to round them up in service. It was called a draft, but it was no more than slavery to a dying political power.

Once the resistance groups and others that were still hopeful for peace understood that doomsday was barking at their heels, they had to make a hard choice, and hid from humanity. A group of five hundred came together and

1

purchased the large island nation, hunkered down, and waited for the smoke to clear. Their hope was that they could return to the world once level heads had prevailed, but every ten years when a small group was sent out into the world they never returned. At some point the leaders decided to stop sending their people out like sheep to the slaughter.

The physical changes happened gradually and unnoticed at first. It was an elder at a meeting that brought up old pictures of humans from a history book that made the Hooni take notice of how drastically different they were from their human ancestors.

That day of acknowledgement is now a national holiday celebrated by the estimated million or so Hooni on the island now called Dayak. The island was renamed that by some of the human scientist who first settled here after its purchase. Dayak was the name belonging to a handful of beautiful native people who still lived primitively near the mountains and remained on the island after it's s sale, lending their knowledge of the native wildlife, and herbal medicine to the new sanctuary civilization that its new owners were making.

Dayak was a breathtakingly gorgeous island. Beaches, rainforest, and mountains gave it a physical aspect that made it feel like the whole world was represented on its back. The group of humans that had secluded themselves there were the smartest and most creative minds of their times. While the rest of the world fell into madness and dystopian ruin, Dayak blossomed. Everyone worked together and shared everything.

Weekly council meetings were partly potluck backyard barbecue style parties and part serious life planning board meetings! In the thousands of years since then, these weekly meetings hadn't changed much. The population had grown to millions of Hooni, that large of a number meant not everyone was there anymore, but everyone was always represented well. So, while Vera sat eating some grilled fish that lady Natuke had once again overcooked she looked around at the hundreds of Hooni and wondered how long she'd have to endure today's meeting. She knew it was an important event and was honored to be chosen out of all the teachers in her area to represent her profession, but she couldn't help being bored to tears at the same time.

She was startled from her boredom by a loud voice saying, "ABSOLUTELY NOT." All eyes darted in the direction of the elder table. There sat a stern-faced Lady Vazeet staring squarely at the Councilman Een, head of correctional punishment for all the Hooni. Her jaw was set and fixed and her furrowed brow showed she meant business. It was rare for a Hooni to raise their voice at all, and most definitely unheard of at civil meetings. Everyhooni scrambled for their seat as if they'd been caught by a mother with their hands in the cookie jar.

The head of council, who was called Zalee quickly called all the eyes to himself as he was forced to start the meeting before schedule.

"Well, I hope everyone has had a productive week, I know we have here at the council offices. Let's jump right into the matters to be discussed and voted on tonight." He said with a false positivity in his voice.

At first all seemed normal, voting for improvements to public play areas were approved, shared farming lands were granted the annual Permission to pull able bodied teenagers from school for harvest week, and new representatives for the engineering board were voted in due to retirement by the former representatives in those slots. The outburst could easily have been swept under the rug and forgotten if Lady Vazeet had remained silent and let the meeting come to a natural close.

However, that was not in her to be silent. She was small, even by Hooni standards. Her thick gray hair had a personality all its own. She'd been the representative for education before moving on to be at the high seat of the elder wisdom council. She'd always been outspoken and quirky, yet very brilliant and kind. No one would have been able to get away with interrupting ZaLee's closing speech other than her!

"I'm sure you've all heard the whispers today about the uprisings within the correctional facility."

Very few Hooni ever committed crimes, there was only one jail on the whole island and within its walls were only about fifty people. They normally worked off their punishment in service to the community and with extensive therapy they always were released back into society, never to offend again.

"We have a group of ten Hooni who have became hard to handle. They are resistant to participate in rebuilding therapies, nor do they complete the jobs they're given. The reason you heard me loudly protesting earlier was because councilman Een was asking each council member, INDIVIDUALLY I might add, which as you all know goes against Hooni way, about his new proposal for dealing with these unusual troublemakers.

"I believe it is wrong, and I oppose it greatly, but as with our traditions I will ask him tell you all, so you can think about it over the following week. Because Hooni do-NOT - decide - things - on - their - own -that - affect - the - rest - of - us." As she said the last line she turned fully towards councilman Een, and punched each word hard and slowly as her eyebrows seemed to raise higher with each word.

Being put on the spot and called out for unHooni like behavior made Een stand up tentatively and address the room.

"As Lady Vazeet has already said, these ten people are dangerous. They show no ability to be rehabilitated, despite the normal proceedings that have worked since the building of the correctional facility. I have thought long and hard about how to handle this. In the last few weeks their attitudes have been causing unrest in otherwise Compliant Hooni working towards release. I fear their behavior would spread like a sickness. I've been reminded of how evil

4

spread amongst our human forefathers that required the creation of our new world in the first place."

Growing impatient with Een, Lady Vazeet unceremoniously snapped, "out with it Een!" He then cleared his throat and spit out his master plan.

"I ask you all to consider expelling them from Dayak, we would not only be removing a budding problem that could threaten our way of life and peace, but we could use them to access the world beyond our shores. They'd be fitted with trackers and cameras. Once they have made their way to the mainland, we could see the world that we have been so curious about."

Een stood silently as the whispers from the crowd started. Head of council, ZaLee, rose to his feet and brought the meeting to an end, but not before saying,

"This proposal is highly theoretical and needs to not be spread amongst the rest of Hoonikind. It may spark fear and unneeded panic. So, I beg you, keep it to yourselves as you think about it over the week and it will be the first topic addressed at the next meeting."

The crowd calmly left the building and acted as if they'd not heard just heard the most disturbing thing in their lives.

Once outside Vera saw her lifelong friend sitting in wait on a bench across the path from where she was standing. There were no vehicles or beast of burden to pull wagons. Other than a large, bearded hog that farmers used to pull small carts along while vegetables were harvested. So, no major roads existed, but beautiful curving walking paths connecting everything.
The two had not seen each other all day. Work had kept them separated. Vera smiled widely and almost ran towards Tallah. They touched hands and began the walk back to the house they shared.

Young women lived in group houses. It made sharing the work at home, in the community and their day jobs run smoother. The house they shared was full of five other Hooni gals but one by one they'd all partnered off and moved to family living pods leaving the two alone. Hooni rarely were alone and the two at first found the house scary and uncomfortable without its normal buzz but now they loved the newfound freedom it brought.

"How was work?" Vera asked. Tallah Rolled her large hazel eyes as she said, "Fine, how was the meeting?" Vera replied with the same answer and eye roll that Tallah had given. Both girls stopped walking and seriously looked at each other's faces for a few seconds then dissolved into giggles. They both knew the answers were bogus, they also knew they couldn't discuss anything out in the open, so they continued to trek home.

It was about a twenty-minute walk. It gave them plenty of time to decompress from work on most days. Vera was head teacher at the local primary school. She had her own class of excited nine-year-old hooni to deal with but also headed all the teacher meetings and was the go to person for any problem in the school. Rarely was discipline an issue with the students, so most problems were about the building itself or event scheduling. She was the youngest to be appointed head teacher in the school's history. It was an honor, and many compared her to Lady Vazeet. Sometimes she didn't know how to take that remark.

Tallah, was a Botanist working with the large farm that grew most of the cultivated food for Dayak. She loved plants and growing things, she often said if her hands weren't dirty by the end of the day she'd not lived.

Their idle conversations came to an abrupt halt. As they rounded the corner, Vera stopped in mid step and yanked Tallah so hard it pulled her back a few inches. The words they had been about to speak were forgotten and both women stood Statue like on the path. There in front of them staring back was a large, clouded leopard. There were only two large animals that could pose a problem on the island, sun bears and these guys.

Neither were common to be seen. The muscles in the leopard's leg twitched and Vera knew he'd not stay still forever, she feared it running their way. In an extremely bold move Vera bounded forward towards the animal screaming and clapping her hands. The leopard turned and ran back towards the jungle past the trail.

Tallah reached out for Vera and hugged her tightly. "That was the bravest, and most stupid thing I've ever seen! What were you thinking?"

Vera let out a heavy sigh, "I was just hoping it would be more afraid of a crazy Hooni than I was of it. We got lucky."

Shaking her head, Tallah and Vera continued onward. "We need to stop at the pod here and let them know that we saw the leopard, and we can alert the head of animal interactions. That way we can all stay safe and be on alert."

Vera nodded and the two turned into the path leading to the pod of houses nearby. All homes in Dayak were on a reverse Cul-de-sac like set up. The homes were in a circle, with all the backyards connected. Sharing backyards forced people to be social and made them work together. It also cut down on secrecy and forced the Hooni to be active members of society.

The five to ten homes which made up the pods had people at the same point in life. Either senior pods, with no kids, pods with young couples and no kids, or pods that had family units with young kids, in turn pods with families that had older kids and teens were common. There were also pods for single females and likewise for males. Which is where Tallah and Vera lived. The head of housing had their hands full.

The pod they'd turned into had seniors. They placed the older Hooni pods nearer to the main hub, or town center so they didn't have to walk as far. Vera knew most of the seniors in this pod so when they were spotted coming down the path they were met with waves and warm smiles. Tallah and Vera made their way around the pod telling each home about the leopard. Luckily the head of animal interaction also lived in this pod. He was noticeably concerned by this news.

"I shouldn't say anything girls," he said in a hushed tone. "But this isn't the first time this month that animals in the area have been out of sorts. We all must keep our guard up. They often know when change is in the air. We may see horrible storms this season."

They nodded. Vera sensed the old man thought more was happening to the animals than just sensing bad weather but she kept her uneasiness to herself.

Once everyone had been informed the two women went back to the main path towards home. They remained on high alert and didn't talk much the rest of the way. Upon entering their house, they both slumped onto chairs in the main room.

"Well, the leopard is officially the best part of my day!" Tallah said in a flat tone. Vera raised one eyebrow which asked, 'how' without words.

"The entire Aquaponics seeding room got upended." She said. Vera snickered and Tallah doubled down,

"No Vera, you don't understand. The head of germination got mad, went yelling about something and knocked all the tray tables full of young plants and flowing water over. Next thing I know he came out into the greenhouse where I was and starting arguments with the staff out there, Vera he struck someone. He's currently sitting in a holding room at the hospital to see if he's had some mental issue!"

Vera sat in shocked silence. Hooni were peaceful, they never raised their voice, they rarely had disagreements. It all had been a harmonious life since the first 500 humans established it. They were very intelligent in how the human brain functions and worked to weed out that primal instinct for aggression. They also built a society around transparency and equality. For someone to behave so blatantly rude was earth shattering.

Vera leaned to the edge of her chair, "lady Vazeet yelled at the meeting today too. There are seemingly unresolvable issues at the correctional center. It was a whole ordeal." She told her the whole story but warned it must not leave them. The two made their way to the kitchen to cook and end their day the same as always, reading books till they fell asleep.

# CHAPTER TWO

The next day the two awoke to the normal chatter of birds outside. On the long walk to the center of town they discussed the upcoming Hooni day festival. It was the first one in their adult life where they didn't have to work a booth. The festival lasted two days, almost the entire population of Dayak came. There was music, storytelling, and food. All of it was free. It was a reward for all the collective hard work by everyhooni. There was no real money on the island in the way that ancient humans had. Everyone who worked had equal share in the food stores, housing was provided, as for specialized items they traded for them.

Tallah and Vera fell into a natural lull in conversation. Silently they walked side by side. Their strides almost matched. Vera was shorter than Tallah, so her steps were always quicker. Every so often she'd half skip to keep up with Tallah. For a Hooni she was tall. Her legs were long, and her body was thin and wispy. Vera was fit and healthy but on her short legs and wide hips Vera found herself in envy of Tallah sometimes.

Despite her short squat appearance Vera had always been quick. Running was a favored way she spent her free time. On weekend mornings before her community activities, she could be found running the paths that extended outward toward the center of the island. Both women loved to go out and explore the mostly uninhabited wild heart of Dayak, but Vera needed those mornings where nothing existed but her feet beating against the earth as her body carried her out of her normal day, even if it was just a couple of hours a week.

Sometimes on their walk to work Vera had to stifle the urge to take off running. It wasn't that Tallah would be angry should she just sprint away, quite the contrary, she found Vera's need to run amusing. It just wouldn't be very adult Hooni like. If the children, she was in charge of during the day saw her running in her dress it may create laughter. Children were allowed to laugh and be happy, but to laugh at someone, especially an adult was considered rude. She needed to maintain her position as professional head teacher and not allow any room for her students to doubt her authority. Hooni were naturally well behaved and civil, but child training was still crucial.

Almost from birth Hooni were taken to nanny houses. It was almost like school but for babies. Every baby was on the same sleep, feeding, and play schedule. When the parents picked them up at the end of the workday the schedule at home was kept unified for the ease of the family and the nanny houses. All medical needs, vaccinations and educational purposes were done for the children while the parents worked for the greater of Dayak. Discipline was also universal among Hooni. Sharing, manners, and calmness were required. Failure to play by the rules resulted in a specific set of actions. First, the misbehaving hooni child was spoken to by the head nanny, or teacher depending upon the age of the child. Then the conversation was continued at home. Atonement was made in the form of self-sacrifice fitting the crime.

A child who didn't share had to give away twice as many things willingly than were not shared to begin with. A child who'd used unkind words had to attend to anyone who cried or was sad for the next week. The list continues in very clear lines of consequences.

Upon the second offense the child was given a prepackaged meal daily for the week. It was nourishment, but bland and devoid of the beautiful flavor and color on the other children's plates. It was meant to show the child that bad behavior separates that Hooni from the rest of the benefits that the group has.

If the child's misbehavior didn't correct almost instantaneously, they were sent to the L.A.B.S. This stood for Learning And Behavior services. Scientists had found that repeated bad behavior in young people was often due to a deficiency which prohibits the brain from making the correlation between

Cause-and-effect. A series of injects were administered and the child was almost never a problem again.

Vera had three cases turned over to the L.A.B.S. At this very minute. It was always something that gutted her when a teacher brought a child on their third strike to her. She felt like the hangmen she'd read about in history books. Back when man punished one another for crimes by committing murder. The whole concept of justified killings turned her stomach. So often she sat holding the hand of the child while awaiting the L.A.B.S. Team to collect them. She wanted to give the child words of encouragement but could find no words, so silence filled the space. Her heart begged her to run and take the child before the L.A.B.S. arrived, but she could not. It was the rule of the island and a necessary event for the smooth future of both the child and Dayak. Rationalizing these facts made it manageable, but she had not ever been able to shake the uneasy feeling in her stomach on those horrible days.

As Vera thought about the children and the injections, she couldn't help but remember her own struggle with obedience, luckily for her, she had a mother who feared having a child not be properly managed. Vera's mother could almost sense when she was going to back talk or otherwise be rude. She'd grab her little hand and squeeze slightly, followed by a conversation when they were alone again.

This in itself was an act of rebellion by her mother, and Vera always wondered why her mother resisted the normal flow of things. Sometimes at night Vera would cry and wonder why she was bad. If something was wrong with her brain to cause her to be opinionated and have the desire to be vocal about it, then shouldn't she be given the injections to correct it. It perpetually worried her little mind.

Thankfully Vera never had a single infraction on her name. If she had, then a position of respect wouldn't have been available to her. Not that the other jobs on Dayak were less than or looked down upon but head teacher was an important role in the community and gained her a seat at the council meetings.

"Vera, where are you going?" Tallah called from behind her. She startled and looked around. She had passed the pathway to the school by about twenty feet. She smiled and sheepishly walked back towards Tallah.

"I was off in my own world I suppose, thanks for catching me." She said in little more than a whisper. The two nodded at each other and parted ways. The farm that Tallah worked at was beyond the main city's hub.

As Vera stepped through the doorway into the school, she looked over her shoulder and took a last glance at Tallah, who was rounding the bend and would be out of sight with a few more steps. She knew that with Tallah alone on the path that she'd be singing. Tallah had an amazingly rich voice. Smiling but still resisting the urge to run Vera pressed into the building and went straight for her classroom.

She always straightened and cleaned the room before leaving it for the day, but with the meeting yesterday she'd rushed out leaving the room a little tossed. Quickly she began to straighten the desk and chairs. She'd just put away the last stack of books as her class filled the room.

They calmly took their seats and stared at Vera. As she began the lesson she yawned. This time of year always had a section devoted to the founding of Dayak. Vera listened to her students as they read aloud from their history books.

"The world had fallen into madness and dark days were all that lay ahead for humans. The air was thick with pollution and the water was too dirty to safely drink. Humans were at war with themselves. Many groups, as well as individuals battled each other over resources, and differences of opinions. Some humans banded together and left the rest of civilization behind. They created a safe world on a large island. This is what we now call Dayak.

"These founding members were the brightest minds of their time. They kept their advanced science and medicine but rejected many other ideas that had been proclaimed as innovative. They no longer made things that hurt the earth. Everything had to be sustainable and reusable.

"Another thing that our ancestors did away with were devices called phones and internet. This was a system so that humans across the planet could speak to one another instantly. It should have been a way to connect mankind and create a global community, but it was instead infested by hate and greed. Leaving humans unproductive and Envious Of each other. Countries as well as individuals fell victim to a "me first" mentality that led to great destruction.

"Just ten years before Dayak was purchased by our beneficiaries atomic Bombs were dropped on the majority of land masses. The world was becoming more unlivable every day. As the main scientist formed their escape plan, they named their team 'omega' an ancient word for 'the end' because that's what they thought was upon them. Every human that was chosen to come and live on Dayak had to have a series of injections and go through an isolation Quarantine before arrival.

"The scientists made sure they didn't bring any existing illnesses to their new world they were creating. The giant ship that they used to bring the original 500 members of 'omega' was later burned to further ensure that no sickness was released onto the island.

"In the first five years of life on Dayak bomber airplanes could still be seen by scouts here on the island. When their notable absence had reached a year duration 'the omega' group held a memorial service for the rest of the world. They knew that they'd narrowly escaped the Annihilation of mankind. They were thankful that no bombs had touched the island.

"In the early years life on Dayak was challenging but thanks to persistence of those intelligent humans we now have the freedom to live in harmony with one another on this bountiful island."

As the last child took his turn reading, a buzz from the back of the room began. It was small at first, the sound of two children talking softly. The volume soon became loud enough that Vera could clearly make out a few words. "That's not nice" and "that's not true." Were among the hubbubs.

Vera held up her hand and cleared her throat. Stopping the boy from reading and redirecting the class's focus to her. Everyone turned back in their seats and away from the two bickering at the back to a respectable position with eyes forward and hands clasped on their desk.

"Please share with the rest of the class what was so important that you felt it was acceptable to interrupt Flynn reading about the founding of Dayak."

A student, named Mirak, from the back of the room rose to her feet. Her shoulder length black hair was tied up with a pretty ribbon except for a few strands that fell towards her face as she started to explain, in an almost too eager voice. Vera extended her hand in a gesture letting the girl know that she had permission to speak.

"Deevid said he wished he could see an airplane drop bomb, and I told him that was horrible."

Before she could even sit down the small boy from the front row asked in his squeaky voice. "What exactly is a 'bomb'?"

In response to being tattled on, Deevid stood up and pleaded his case. "I don't want anyone hurt, I just think it'd be neat to see. Mirak is acting like I'm killing hooni!"

By this point the entire room was filled with the sound of every child talking over each other. Vera looked around the room, never had she ever heard any interest in a violent act by anyone her entire life. The child obviously didn't mean any harm with the statement, but it still sent chills down her spine.

The thought of a hooni killing another hooni was unheard of. As Vera clapped her hands to regain control of the room once more, Deevid raised his voice to a full yell and said something unintelligible towards Mirak. Even though she didn't know what he'd said she knew it was his second strike.

She took him by the hand and once the room was calmly working on their math sheets, she took him to the isolation room. Where she proceeded to give him the normal Speech that came with such an infraction. "...and you know you'll be having the L.A.B.S. Prepackaged lunch for a while. I'm sorry but when you act in unhooni like ways then you don't get to enjoy the benefits of being hooni.

Deevid hung his head and almost cried as he was led back to his seat in the classroom. Which she moved to an obscure corner of the room so he couldn't interact with the classroom.

Vera pointed to the sign above the blackboard and obediently the class read it in unison. "A well-formed society never fails, we're stronger together - out of many we are one."

As the words slipped past her lips a cold shiver washed down her. As Hooni day got closer her mind always wondered about how they'd successfully lived peacefully when the humans who'd come before them had failed. Now a child in her midst casually mentions wanting to see airplanes drop bombs as if it was normal.

Sometimes she looked at her peaceful civil world with pride, but sometimes she wondered what they were giving up for that peace. Perhaps they weren't even aware of what was missing because no one knew anything different.

Vera had seen the horrible photos from war that were in her advanced human studies books that she had taken in her higher educational classes to become a teacher. She knew this child knew nothing of what bombs did, nor did he know what a gun was. Or how humans came in multiple skin colors, and how much division that had caused. It seemed no matter how much humans had, they always wanted more and never did they have enough to share with those who had not been able to get it.

Yes, she wondered about what pieces were missing on Dayak, but she shoved that question back down into the depths of her heart. She knew she wasn't too old to be taken by the L.A.B.S.. Should it ever be found out that she held ideas outside of the normal patterns of society she would be stripped of her job title and sent to work in a more strenuous job.

Vera most feared being put to work fishing. Many hooni fell victim to the saltwater crocodiles living in the rivers that cut through Dayak.

No matter what job the hooni had, they still got the same share of food, and same home as everyone else did. However, Vera often wondered if the more grueling jobs shouldn't get more food. Surely, they needed more calories to work that hard. Not to mention they had to rise earlier and go to bed later to be able to get into and out of the jungle for work since it was farther than local jobs. Aptitude tests every five years of life were compiled at age 20 to determine what hooni was best suited for which job.

When Vera was five her first test showed she was suited for harvesting work. Her mother found this out because she peeked into the test results. Vera's mother was a scientist at the L.A.B.S. She would have been immediately released for abusing her position had someone known.

The changes her mother made to her daily life were subtle but obviously they changed her enough so that the end results were teacher. She should never have messed with fate, nor should Vera have ever known about any of this. However, her mother, 'Kai', had come to her one night before her last aptitude test in a panic.

She'd confessed things that she'd done to keep Vera from being taken to the L.A.B.S. As a child, and the way she'd made sure that Vera didn't have to be placed into an exhausting physical job in the future. Kai had tears soaking her shirt by the time she was done. She fell asleep in Vera's bed that night. Tired from the weight of the knowledge that she'd been so unHooni all these years. Her mother kept saying, we're different. Something is on the horizon, but I can't make it out. Vera never got to ask any follow up questions after that night. Her mother died at work the next month.

The remainder of Vera's day went about as generically as any other day. Lessons, lunch, and the other normal workings of a school. When she had finished her day and found herself once again cleaning up the classroom in preparation for next morning, she was pleasantly surprised when Koi walked in.

He politely tapped on the open door to announce his presence. He had startled Vera once before, resulting in him being shoved backwards over a desk, and from then on, he made sure she heard him coming. She grinned at Koi, she had seen him walk up to the door. It was obvious they'd made eye contact and the warning knock wasn't needed. Nonetheless be it in satire or politeness he had knocked anyway.

Smiling he sat down backwards in a student's chair facing her. "I had the most bizarre question in class today." He said without even saying hello.

"This girl asked 'if humans still existed would they kill us if they could find us? I didn't even know how to answer that I just told her not to talk of horrible things, and that she knows we're safe."

"I had to give a student his second warning and food bricks today. I win the contest for most bizarre day." She responded as she sat down facing him.

"I had no knowledge that we were in competition, I'll have to start trouble tomorrow." He said a tad louder than he'd intended.

Vera immediately shushed him. "We both know we're joking when we talk like that, but it wouldn't be looked on favorably should anyone else hear it. Besides you know the teacher next to me is as strict as any hooni can be about being proper. She'd love nothing more than to report me and take this position as head teacher and council lady."

Koi looked around in all directions, got up and walked to the open door. He glanced up one side and then the other, once he was sure the hall was clear he walked quickly back to where Vera sat and kissed her passionately but quickly.

"If we are going to be unhooni I may as well enjoy it." Vera's heart leapt in her chest as she felt a flush of heat sweep across her neck and face.

Koi and Vera's mothers had worked together at the L.A.B.S. and they'd grown up in the same pods as young kids. They'd been moved to separate pods as teens, yet their mothers remained close friends. Vera and Koi were often caught listening in on hushed conversations their mothers would have over coffee.

"Are we going to officially put our name in the couple registering system anytime soon?" He asked. "We haven't even told Tallah!" She answered. "What are we waiting on?" He sounded almost childlike as the last note of the question hit the air.

She shook her head and looked seriously at him. "Something feels unstable on Dayak, and it makes me nervous to do anything right now."

"You're sounding like our mothers" he said as his shoulders dropped.

She too could sense a familiarity in her wariness when she spoke about how different everything was getting lately. Koi wasn't wrong, it was very reminiscent of the way their mothers would talk leading up to the time just before their death.

The two women had been found huddled together in their workstation unresponsive. It was later determined that an accidental spill of hazardous chemicals by one of them had caused their death. This explanation never set well with Vera, but she accepted the answer. There was no reason to doubt the head of L.A.B.S., if anyone after all should know about chemicals it would be her. Lotta no longer headed the L.A.B.S. But had a seat at the elder table of knowledge in the council. Her replacement was none other than her own son, this was rare for a hooni to have the same job as a parent, let alone fill the same roll his parent had had, but it fell this way for Lotta and Lorn.

She'd raised him and his sisters as a single mother after her husband went mad and was admitted into the infirmary until his death some many years later. Vera had overheard Kai and Koi's mom 'Naandi' saying that Lotta had the staff working on an antidote for what she claimed was a jungle virus that her husband had gotten from the Proboscis monkeys. Kai also had said that 'it's strange that dozens of people in connection with Lotta have this mysterious illness that's never been heard of before.'

"I know." Vera said as she reached out and held Koi's hand for a split second before looking up to note the time. "I have to scramble to meet Tallah at the crossroads. We have an errand to run before dinner."

"Travel safe." He said warmly. She stopped short of the door and rushed back towards him,

"Oh yeah I almost forgot, I saw a leopard on the way home yesterday, just walked out of the jungle and stared at Tallah and Me like an easy meal. Luckily it was scared of me! I chased it off! Be careful walking home and warn others. Bye for real this time!"

Then just like that she was gone. Out of the room and out of the building before Koi could fully process what'd been said. He stood up and looked around the room. A few chairs had been left out, which he slid back under their correct desk and closed the door. He couldn't help but grin all the way to his bachelor pod.

He truly Loved Vera. Her mind was sharp as a tack. Koi and Vera thought very similarly, they had the same off-color humor that wasn't very acceptable among other hooni. They, like their mothers before them were masquerading as normal, when in reality they tended to be outside of the norm. It was in this that they clicked with each other where they didn't with most others.

# CHAPTER THREE

Tallah had her back towards Vera as she quickly walked up the path toward their decided meeting place, a crossroads of their two jobs. Vera could see by Tallah's body language and tapping foot that she'd been waiting on her longer than she'd have liked to.

When she neared Tallah she got straight to apologizing. "I'm here, I'm here! I'm sorry I had another whopper of a day, followed by a last-minute visit from Koi."

Tallah started walking as Vera reached her and the two turned down the path towards the fishing stands near the large river on their side of the island. After that they'd stop by the foraging center. They would pick up this half of their food shares today and tomorrow they'd gather the rest at the farm and the home store. This was the only drawback the two girls had found to living virtually alone in the bachelorette house. They weren't able to carry all the items home at once, so they often had to break their gathering runs into a few trips. It made the work week longer but the two enjoyed the walking with one another.

"My day was mostly uneventful, just damage control after the incident yesterday. The Aquaponics room had been completely restored to normal and we were busy pulling plants from our grow rooms to fill those trays. I had some spare time to go check on my hybrid mushroom experiment. As you know absolutely no one has been able to manipulate the gnome of any mushroom to create the giant sizes like what we can do with other food for the shares. Well..." she stopped and clamped her lips together in sheer excitement. The unbridled joy wanted to rush out as she struggled to hold it in for dramatic effects.

"The Laetiporus sulphureus has begun to fruit and the fingers of this fungus are giant! I am going to wait a few more days before I show the head of the farm. I know I should have gone and gotten him today, but so much can go wrong. I don't want to get his hopes up. Plus, if they decide my experiment needs to be moved over to the science wing of the farm I'll never get to see it grow. Oh, Vera is that selfish of me?"

Sometimes questions like that from Tallah shook her inside, deep down the notion that the group was to always come before the individual felt wrong to her.

"Tallah, it's absolutely not selfish. It's very interesting and you're very intelligent to come up with this plan to make more food for every hooni to enjoy. That's doing what's best for the group so no, not selfish!"

Tallah swelled with pride and a smile spread across her face. Vera let Tallah bask in her much deserve glory before beginning to retell about the second strike for the kid in her class.

"It's just that there's been so many instances in the school this year. It concerns me. Anyhoo, don't let us forget to go look at those flowers past the fish stands please! Tallah nodded and the two could now see and smell the fishing stand. The foraging stalls were farther past the fish, so they decided to press on to it first and get the fish on the way back.

At the foraging stalls they handed over their food cards and were given a basket a piece. The items available here were always a surprise and could vary greatly depending on what was available. They'd fill their baskets and take the things home in them. Leaving the baskets by their door to be picked up by one of the hooni who worked wherever the basket had come from.

Tallah's eyes lit up as she picked up wild mushrooms, it caused Vera to snicker a little. The grow rooms at the farms had never put much attention to growing mushrooms. They were to readily available in the jungles and the foraging crews kept up with the demand for them. The farm had mostly been used to grow foods that had been brought by the omega team from the outside world.

When she proposed her ideas to the head of the farm to let her play with the wild things, she had to ask permission all the way up to the elder hooni council. It was a big deal. Head of council ZaLee had accepted it but scolded her in the same breath for not being fulfilled in the work that she already had.

Tallah and Vera filled their baskets and headed over to let the woman weigh it. It didn't matter what they got; it was by weight. So as the woman placed their baskets on the scale Vera studied the body paints, stains and tattoos that decorated her skin. The woman had a reddish-brown handprint on her neck, with yellow dots leading from it down to her collarbone. Her face had green flecks across it, it appeared that paint had been flicked off a brush onto her face, giving the appearance of green freckles.

The foragers, and hunters always decorated their bodies in these ways. It was said to have started as a way to camouflage themselves and turned into a part of their identity. Some very strict hooni claimed it went against the norm and should be banned. Luckily lady Vazeet always comes to their defense, that it's 'their normal, which makes it normal for hooni kind'. Lady Vazeet after all had come from the foraging pods. It's rare that foraging families have children who leave and work in the community proper, but it does happen.

Leaving the foraging stand the women thanked the lady at the stall and went towards a small foot path into the jungle where they'd been watching a beautiful flower patch. The blooms were gorgeous and Vera and Tallah had been sketching them at different stages of their development.

Just before they could round the corner to the flowers, an angry sounding voice caught Vera's ear. She grabbed Tallah and pulled her behind the large tree that was nearby. Tallah immediately scrunched her face and in a very agitated voice exclaimed, "Vera, what in the world are you..." but she didn't get to finish that question because Vera clapped her hand over Tallah's mouth. The shock of Vera being physical with Tallah was enough to scare them both. The two stood wide eyed looking at each other,

Vera jerked her head to the side and mouthed the word, 'listen' Vera lowered her hand and they both now directed their attention to the sound of the voice, which was much more clear now than it had been at first. A familiar males voice was obviously fussing and angry at another male, that neither of them knew. When Vera gathered the courage to look around the tree, she saw the unmistakable profile of Lorn, head of the L.A.B.S.

"I don't care what it takes, I need five more monkeys and the plants on my list by no later than day after tomorrow!" Lorn's voice was gruff and hushed. Giving it the sound of hot air escaping a crevasse in the earth.

"Lorn, I'm doing the best I can! The more that you request monkeys the harder they are to find. It means I'm constantly after them, it makes them move their troop frequently and they are becoming so leery of me it's almost impossible to catch them. I'm having to rely on traps alone and they're even getting wise to those now.

"The plants are almost as complex to get because we've exhausted them. They can't regrow as fast as you're using them. Which pushes me deeper into the jungle where I spook the monkey troops again and again." The unnamed hunter tells Lorn with a warm deep voice that seems to resonate off the trees.

"Keep your voice down, I don't care how difficult it is for you, just make sure it's done. If not, you won't like what I replace the monkeys with." Lorn hisses

The hunter draws up to his full size, looks down at Lorn and in his same deep rich voice says, "I have half a mind to go to the head of council about your 'needs' Lorn!"

Lorn immediately pokes a finger into the hunter's chest, "Don't you have young children?"

The hunter exhales and sinks backward. "I'll get you what you ask, Lorn." He turns and walks away from Lorn directly into the depths of the jungle.

The two women hold their breath and hug tightly onto the backside of the tree as Lorn walks by on the nearby path. He's heading back into the fishing market and foraging stall area.

Once he's out of sight, the two women crumple onto the ground. Tallah is visibly shaking. They try to gather themselves, and Vera whispers,

"We have to walk out of these woods like we heard nothing, do you understand? We go get fish; we go home! We do NOT talk about this until we're alone! If we see Lorn, we gotta act normal! Something is very, very wrong here."

"I don't know if I can, I'm scared."

Tallah replied. "You don't have a choice." Vera said in a flat tone as she pulled Tallah to her feet and the two returned to the footpath.

Her feet felt disconnected from her body. She tried to find a normal pace but no matter how slow or fast, it seemed awkward. Her mind was going a million different directions and none of them were making any sense. As they exited the path and stepped into the clearing, she scanned around for Lorn. She wanted to make sure he wasn't skulking nearby watching the path. To her relief he was nowhere to be seen. She unwound her arm from Tallah's.

The two were still intertwined in fear. Seeking comfort, as well as comforting the other. It would draw attention if the two continued to walk that way. Physical contact in public was another thing that was 'unHooni' in nature.

Quickly they picked out enough things at the fish stalls to meet their second basket's weight requirements. Fresh water shrimp, mud bugs, and some whole fish were quickly wrapped in large banana leaves. Fish doesn't keep long, even in their cool spring houses beside the main house. So this basket was lighter than the foraging ones.

Randomly amid Walking home, Vera began talking about the flowers they'd been sketching. She was noting color and how the bees had been dusted with pollen. Tallah kept looking at her as if she'd grown a second head. Vera was able to catch Tallah's eyes, she narrowed her eyebrows extremely and darted her eyes to the side. Tallah followed the eye line and saw none other than Lorn standing at the fork towards their pod. Understanding what Vera was doing she quickly picked up her end of the conversation about the flowers. When they passed him, they continued the rouse perfectly.

Then he called for her. "Vera."

The hair on their neck stood up as they stopped and waited for him to catch up with them. Never had the need to run so desperately pulled at her. They both stood stoically though.

"Hi Tallah," he nodded as he addressed her before turning to Vera. "I was on my way to your place, I wanted to see if you wanted to come eat with me at the café after this week's meeting?"

Before Vera could reply, it was Tallah who came to the rescue. "We're finishing our projects to be able to trade for hooni day and that's our only available time."

Lorn looked from Tallah to Vera, obviously being turned down hadn't crossed his mind. Vera saw something flash across his eyes that made her blood run cold.

"I can meet you tomorrow after school for coffee though." She said. Relief washed across him.

"Sounds great. I can't wait. Thank you." He smiled as he bid them goodbye and walked away.

Once out of earshot Tallah said, "I had you free and clear what the hey!"

Vera shook her head slightly and didn't answer until she opened their front door. Once inside she made vomit sounds and shook from head to toe as if she'd stepped into a spider's web.

"I got the feeling that he'd never stop asking, I didn't want to make him think I was avoiding him either. I'm not sure why but I HAD to agree to meet him. I just felt it in my bones."

Tallah didn't know how to respond. They grabbed one another and hugged tightly.

".. but listen Tallah, you find Koi and meet me at the crossroads one hour after schools out. That will give me enough time for coffee, and you two will be my excuse to leave. Should he escort me out of the café you two will provide confirmation to my excuse. Not to mention I don't want to walk home alone, nor do I want you coming home completely by yourself either!"

"What did we stumble upon Vera?" She asked and the quake in her voice could be felt deep inside.

"I don't know for sure, but I've been thinking about what Lorn said all the way home. This may sound crazy, but I think he's doing some kind of experiment using the monkeys. It would have to be something that's not approved by the council, otherwise he wouldn't have been threatened by the hunters mention of telling the council. Also, the monkeys would be provided by proper methods. Not by bullying someone in the jungle."

Tallah's put her hands over her face, "he told the hunter he wouldn't like what he'd use in place of the monkeys if he didn't comply. That's seriously not Hooni! We should report this."

Vera reached out and put her hands on Tallah's shoulders, forcing her to raise her face and meet her gaze. "This is definitely NOT Hooni, and we definitely can't report it. I know that it's hard for you to not follow rules, but Tallah we aren't safe, we can NOT, breathe anything about this.... except to...

Koi." Her voice trailed off as she looked out the side window. Their pod was close enough to the bachelor pod that she could see Koi's window from there. The light was on. She got hopeful and told Tallah to lock the door behind her and not open it until she returned.

She was out of the door before Tallah could protest. She stayed to the shadows and snuck around to Koi's window. She didn't want to go to the door and alert the whole house. Unlike her and Tallah, his house was full of young people. She began tapping softly, but frantically against the windowpane.

Finally he opened the curtains. When he saw her, he smiled, but that faded quickly. He recognized the fear in her face and climbed out the opened the window.

"Something bad happened Koi. Give me a ten-minute head start and come to my house. Don't be seen."

He grabbed her and drew her close. "Okay Vera, okay. Go I'm on my way."

She turned and ran as fast as she could. Still taking great care to not be seen.

When she got to her door she knocked with the same soft, and frantic manner that she'd done with Koi's window. Tallah opened and closed the door quickly as Vera passed through it.

"Okay, what's going on? What does Koi have to do with this?" She begged of Vera.

"Look Tallah, it's been something he and I never really talked about, but our moms suspected that Lorn's mom, 'Lotta' was doing something very unhooni. They were concerned about a major thing at the L.A.B.S. before they BOTH turned up dead. You must promise that no matter how bad what we're about to talk about, or how unhooni any of this becomes... promise that you're on my side. We must stick together. Or mine and Koi's mom won't be the last to die mysteriously."

Tallah just looked at her helplessly. Vera knew that what she was asking was sure to cause an 'internal conflict' within her.

"I know I'm asking you to go against what we've been told our whole life, but we won't have a life to worry about if I can't trust you."

At that moment Koi tapped on the door. Tallah nodded her allegiance as she turned to open the door for Koi. Koi entered the house and wrapped Vera in his arms. He looked up and saw Tallah standing beside them. He couldn't help himself and pulled her into the hug. Something inside him just said both women needed to feel safe for the moment. Tallah didn't struggle but allowed the peace to fill the space. Strangely it calmed them and brought a unity to the room.

Koi and Tallah sat down at the kitchen table while Vera disappeared to the bedroom. When she returned, she had a large wooden box with a complicated lock on the side. She sat it down in the center of the table.

Koi sighed almost as if he was relieved. "Vera, have you started thinking about this thing again? Is this what's wrong? I was genuinely worried coming over here!" He looked from Tallah to Vera. "Oh goodness you told Her I suppose. Great, exactly what we'd said we would never do..." his voice grew angrier with each word as he proceeded to scold Her.

Vera was so overcome with frustration that she slammed her hands down on the table hard. The noise made Tallah and Koi both jump.

"Koi, shut your face!" She snapped. "No, I haven't shown her the box, but The box is a must do at this point, but first things first, in the jungle today we saw Lorn, and the man was unhinged!" She threw her hands into the air in a very unhooni like fashion bringing them down in a clenched first to strike the table again.

Vera glanced at Tallah and was about to look away and continue talking when she was forced to do a double take. Jerking her face back towards Tallah she saw that she was standing up with her back to the kitchen door. Her hand was behind her, and the doorknob gripped tightly in her fist at the small of her back.

"Tallah." Vera said as she got closer to her.

Tallah's large silver eyes widened and the sound of the doorknob clicking caused an explosive reaction from Koi and Vera. The two lept out and grabbed Tallah. Vera wrapped her arms around her thin body and sat down hard. Pulling Tallah into her lap on the floor in the process. She instinctively folded her legs over top of Tallah's pinning them below hers. Vera was very thankful for her muscular thick legs at this moment.

Koi grabbed her from the front and put his hand over her mouth. "Don't scream, don't make a sound." Koi said in as soothing a voice as he could.

Vera took over the conversation. "Tallah remember I just told you that I need your allegiance and I promised you I'd explain, do NOT freak out. You know me, Koi let her mouth loose."

Koi did as he was told but didn't move his hands far just in case they needed to be reapplied.

"No way, let me up. You two are sick. Just like the man at work that got angry and yelled. They took him to L.A.B.S. Hospital. There's obviously something going around, and you both have it. I'm going to get help. It's okay, ... it's okay." Tallah said in a very scared voice.

Koi shook his head and sat down in front of her. "Vera she's never gonna get it. This is pointless and you've opened a can of worms that we can't put back!"

"No Koi." She said as she rolled her eyes. "She's capable of understanding I believe what she saw today can't be reasoned away. She's in danger and frankly we all are."

She loosened her grip on Tallah's arms.

"Tallah, getting angry, having big emotions, these things aren't 'unhooni', and whatever causes us to not be able to do it, THATS what's 'unhooni' there's a lot that happens at the L.A.B.S. That we're not allowed to know! Hooni are supposed to be peaceful, generous, communal, and transparent! The fact that something is going on that we don't know about is a contradiction of the very thing that they claim makes us Hooni!... look I know this is confusing, but I know for a fact that you know what you heard in the jungle today was WRONG! If you don't understand anything else right now, please Tallah, hold onto that. You saw something bad today, Koi and I kind of understand about this bad thing. We promise to keep you safe, but you have to be 100% loyal."

Vera looked up at Koi. "We have to do more than kind of understand this stuff now. It's gotten worse."

She redirected back to Tallah. "We're going to trust you. Please trust us in return. Even if you don't understand. Trust us, because If you don't, we will be killed, it's that serious."

Vera felt the muscles in Tallah's body soften. As she did this, Vera exhaled and let go of her. Koi was less trusting and watched her tentatively. All three made their way to chairs at the table. Tallah smoothed her hair back into place and Vera straightened her shirt. They sat almost in stalemate for a few minutes. Each watching for a sign of crazy in the other.

After several tense minutes had passed, Vera told Koi the entire conversation they'd overheard in the jungle. When Koi glanced at Tallah she would nod in confirmation as if her seconding the story meant she was 'IN'. Koi

32

was shocked that Lorn had threatened a hunter in that way, "what could he be doing with monkeys? Unless there really is a sickness that comes from them. Could they still not know how to control it, 'if' that's what this is about." He half asked, half monologued to Vera.

"Sickness, from monkeys?" Tallah asked.

Koi told her the story of how Lorn's dad was admitted into the hospital wing at L.A.B.S. Years ago, "he was supposed to be very sick. Lotta didn't even let anyone but her see him. She was worried about it being contagious. A fourth the staff were pulled from their normal jobs to work on this mystery illness.

"However, no one was allowed to tell anyone. Lotta told them it could 'start a panic.' So, everyone did as they were told. Despite having very little to go on. We sat up at night and listened to our moms talk about it. The two of them had been set to work on a genetic aspect of it. They talked about it being radical to try and alter genetic coding and neural networks to stop a simple illness. As soon as Lotta's husband died, our moms work vanished.

"As, unhooni it may have been... our moms kept duplicates of everything they documented. They also kept notes on Lotta and some other things. They snuck it all out and kept it at home. In that box" he said as he pointed to the center of the table.

"They knew something larger was going on. Major issues. Vera and I don't understand it all. We can't open the box. Never have. We simply know what we overheard from our moms. The two of them designed that lock on the box. We've tried to get into it for what has felt like a lifetime since their death. No luck."

Vera leaned forward to touch the box while picking up where Koi had left off. "It's more than just that Tallah. Our moms had a great mistrust for the L.A.B.S. Despite working there. They did .... a lot of things raising us that aren't okay by Hooni standards. We had anger, disobedience, boundless curiosity, and things like that. Our mothers hid it. Talked to us a lot and kept anyone else from ever finding out.

"We were never given the meal replacement packages, or the injections. We don't know *why* that is either. Our mothers never told us. All we knew is we had to be careful not to act abnormal at school. It was difficult sometimes to not be opinionated with other students and even adults. Luckily, we managed. Our mothers taught us how to be good Hooni, I don't feel like we're different from anyone most of the time, but sometimes I feel very set apart."

Tallah sat still, soaking up all the information before speaking. "You're right, I don't understand all of this. The fact that you two haven't been through the normal steps and injections that you should have had, bothers me. I never had those either, but it's because I only ever had one strike. Although, the fact that you're my friends, and I truly know you, it makes me more concerned that you're fine without them and we were told it was Necessary.

"That makes me suspicious, for which I'm instantly filled with guilt over being suspicious of the elder Hooni. I'm sorry I almost ran away. I won't anymore. You can trust me. I want to know what is being kept from me, from all hoonikind. About that lock... I bet I can open it." She smiled at the two of them.

Vera chuckled as Koi raised his eyebrows in disbelief. "She's amazing at puzzles and codes."

Before Tallah could touch the box, Koi picked the conversation back up.

"We need a game plan to deal with Lorn. I seriously doubt he just suddenly wants to court you, Vera! Not that you're not wonderful, it's just the timing is too perfect. He must have thought he saw you two exiting the jungle and got nervous. You're going to have to really chat up the flower sketching aspect. Sell it hard. In no way can you be alone with him. I don't trust him. Never have. I won't even stand close to him myself at social events."

"You're not wrong." Vera agreed.

"It's going to be a delicate dance at the Café tomorrow. You two will be my escape plan. I already told Tallah what I'm going to need from y'all." Vera filled him in on the two of them waiting at the crossroads and being her excuse, and escort home. The three talked late into the night. Koi slinked back to his house at the bachelor pod. The women were able to get some uneasy sleep before it was time to get ready for work.

# CHAPTER FOUR

On the way out of the door that morning, the two paused, grabbed each other's hand and gave a quick squeeze. Stepping out into the sun they both felt different. Each face they passed and nodded a greeting to made Tallah a little sick inside.

"I know things, they don't know, and they should. I don't like secrets Vera. I hope we solve this quickly; I even more so hope that it's so small I can forget it and be relieved of this feeling inside." She said softly when the road was empty of all but the two of them.

"Me too Tallah, but I sadly I don't think anything about this is 'small' I think we're just scraping the surface of this."

As they got closer the crossroads where they'd have to split up to head to their different jobs, they saw a beautiful bird in the road that normally wasn't seen amid the busy hubs that were full of Hooni.

"I bet this bird, and our leopard we saw are venturing down into our areas because that hunter is spooking wildlife in the heart of Dayak. They're upsetting the balance of the whole world here." Tallah said softly but with an anger underneath the words.

That little hint of anger in her voice gave Vera hope. Even perfect Hooni may still have a fight inside them. They may all need it sooner rather than later.

"You're scary smart Tallah. I hadn't even thought about it, but You're right!" Vera said.

They bid each other a good day and each secretly hoped the other would be safe while they were apart. Vera watched Tallah until she was out of sight. Normally she did that because she was avoiding actually going into the building to begin her workday. Today though she was genuinely paying attention to her friend, she was worried for her. She was suddenly startled so badly that she jumped and yelled a little bit.

"What are you doing Vera?" A female voice asked right in her ear.

She never even heard her fellow teacher, 'Olive' come up behind her. The woman was a stickler for the rules and always nosey.

"I was watching Tallah." Vera said as she tried to calm her breathing back to normal from the surprise jump scare.

"Why are you watching your housemate?" She asked full of busybody inquisition.

"Because we saw a leopard on the path this week, and I'd like to keep my housemate rather than her end up as lunch. She's doesn't always pay attention to her surroundings, so I was just watching out for her." Vera smiled while she turned to face the lady. She was happy to put in that Tallah was less than observant. It felt crazy to be laying lies down but she knew she had to do everything possible to protect Tallah. This Hooni would be one of the first that Lorn would come to if he set out to find information out on Vera and Tallah.

"Happy day", she said as she walked away from Olive.

Once inside her classroom she began writing the days lesson on the board. She had reached the last line as her class came in. They were calm, as always, they took their seats and immediately began to copy the information from the board. The training they received in the nanny pods as small children was very evident.

Vera looked around the room. She wondered if any of her students were hiding abstract thoughts like she'd been as a kid. She doubted since she spent every day with them and knew them so well, but she still couldn't help but wonder. As her eyes moved from one little hooni face to another she noted how all of them were so similar. Hair was the only real difference. Due to the mix of the different races from the omega team, the skin tones were fairly uniformed.

Hues varied some but it was the hair that still showed the uniqueness. Reds, browns, black, and even blond could be seen. Although blond was less common. Some of her students had dreadlocks, some had long loose hair, others had neat braids. Some had short haircuts. Hooni took pride in their hair. It was always neat and clean, no matter the style. The hunters and gatherers often sported shaved sections and beads adorning their locks. Kids hair couldn't be as radical. In school no one was to know what pods they came from. It was one more form of unity among the Hooni. So that Everyhooni had the same opportunities and childhood the goal was that, if they were raised the same, they'd be the same as adults.

As she looked across the back row she was puzzled. One of her students was missing. This never happened. Hooni were rarely sick, she knew instantly it was Deevid who was absent.

"If anyone knows where Deevid is, please come talk to me." Quickly she added, "maybe you normally see him, or someone who knows him on your walk to school, or if anyone heard anything while playing or gathering your food shares yesterday that may be helpful."

She knew she couldn't do anything to let anyhooni's pod be given up publicly, but she was on the verge of panic inside as to where this child was at.

For a few seconds no one moved. Finally, a small boy stood up nervously and walked to her desk. He looked at his toes and began to speak. "Deevid is gone."

Vera told him to "hold on a moment" and she stood and led the boy into the hallway. She walked across the hall to where Koi's room stood empty of students. His morning time was when his students went to their extra class, so she knew it was the only safe place to speak. Plus, she wanted him to hear this firsthand.

"Okay, Hugo, please tell me what you mean by 'Deevids' gone'" lucky for her Koi followed along quickly and didn't need to be told what was going on.

Hugo stuttered with an obvious case of nerves before telling them, "Deevid's house was visited last night by the L.A.B.S. workers. I heard that he was angry when he got home, and someone to report it. His mom didn't know yet he'd already gotten a strike at school I guess, because I saw her crying as she took laundry off the line in the backyard of our pod. He licked his lips as he stopped talking. "But Don't tell anyone I saw her cry. My parents and some others say if we cry over kids going to L.A.B.S. they may come get 'us' too." He looked up. Fear flashed in his young face.

"Thank you, Hugo. You've been helpful. We won't tell you said that, you also shouldn't tell anyone we asked about Deevid." Koi said in his strong teacher's voice.

Hugo and Vera quickly went back to their own classroom. They both shook their head and exchanged worried glances as she walked out of his open door.

The day seemed to speed forward. Drawing Vera closer to her much feared coffee date. When the last student left, Koi nearly ran into the room, closing the door behind him.
"Is it just me, or are they pulling kids sooner, for smaller offenses, particularly from the hunter gatherer pods?" He asked in a single breath.

"You're absolutely right, I've been worried about it lately, but I've tried hard to push it out of my mind. I can't ignore it anymore. Our moms weren't crazy, and neither are we. I'm going to get to the bottom of this one way or another Koi, I'm serious. Not only are these kids being taken more readily, but did you hear Hugo? He said adults are talking about it and crying over it. That means we're not the only ones who don't think in 'proper Hooni' fashion."

He quickly jerked his head up as her words hit him like a ton of bricks. He'd not even thought about that. Looking from her to the clock on the wall. He let out a huge sigh and hugged her.

"I'll tidy your room; you have to get to the café quickly. Be safe, I'll see you in about 45 minutes or so at the crossroads."

Vera got up and left even though she wanted to stay, or better yet run away and hide in a cave for the rest of her life. She let her mind play as she walked to the café. Wondering about what was going on lended itself to an idea that was linked to the MOST unhooni like thing, it was selfishness.

An overwhelming feeling of helplessness and responsibilities threatened to drown her. 'It was too much for one little Hooni' she thought. It also wasn't fair that it was her job to figure this all out. Why did her mother have to set her apart? If she'd had the injections, she'd be ignorantly happy today. If the same had been done to Koi, the two would probably be married by now.

She had almost made herself sick to her stomach when the café came into view. It was one of only places for Hooni to eat. You had to plan out your food card to be able to do it. The food you ate at the café had to be subtracted from the total amount of food you got from the fish stalls, hunting/foraging stands and the farms. The exemptions were that water was free to anyhooni. Coffee was also given freely to members of the council tables. She and Tallah came here once a week. Seeing the building was normally something that made her happy. It was a beautiful, rounded building. The kitchen was in the center, and it was all open air. At a table near the edges with its ornate railing she saw Lorn sitting in wait for her.

When she neared the table, he stood and smiled. She returned his smile and he sat again as she took her seat. Sitting across from him she couldn't help but think that this otherwise unsuspecting hooni was one in the same with who she'd seen threatening someone in the jungle just the day before. He began with the normal formalities, asking about how her day, work, and home were. She gave basic polite answers and returned similar questions to him. Vera was beginning to feel like this was a normal, boring attempt at a date until Lorn finally got down to it.

"The upcoming council meeting has a very important vote to be made. It's been weighing heavily on my mind. I do not think setting those inmates into a boat bound for unknown land is acceptable. I'm going to propose that those causing trouble be turned over to the L.A.B.S. I believe they're sick and it's our Hooni duty to help them, not cast them aside." He said in a sincere voice. "Will you vote with me?"

Had she not known what she knew about him, she may have believed him to have good intentions and been inclined to discuss this matter. In all honesty she hadn't thought much about the problem Hooni at the detention center. She'd been a little preoccupied. However, knowing what she did, she took the opportunity to have the upper hand.

"Lorn, I'm afraid our talking about council matters outside of the meeting hall is forbidden. It's against the rules and I'm going to have leave now before I'm forced to report you. Thank you for the conversation and if you'll excuse me, I must go paint with Tallah for our trading items in order to be done by Hooni day. Good day, Lorn. Safe travels home." She said. When she stood Lorn Shook his head slightly and returned the "safe travels" phrase as is customary for goodbyes.

With each step away from the table Vera felt stronger. Once she'd made it out of sight distance from the café and was on the path towards the crossroads, she couldn't contain herself. She broke into a full run. It was pure unadulterated bliss. Not only had she not been cornered and threatened by Lorn, but she was able to shame him, layer on her Hooni tendencies and ethics which would further throw him off her trail should anything else arise. Plus, she now knew without a shadow of a doubt that Lorn was doing some type of experiment on those monkeys, and he wasn't above using Hooni to experience on. She had to make sure he didn't get to bring those in question to the L.A.B.S., but how she wasn't sure. She was not even out of breath as she ran up to where Koi and Tallah stood waiting for her.

"I'm safe, we're all safe. For now, at least. I'll tell you both everything when we're back at the house. If you guys don't mind walking home together, I really would like to run the rest of the way. I have to get out this energy and I'd like the time to think also." She said in more of a matter-of-fact way than an actual question.

Koi and Tallah both agreed. Knowing that the run was important to Vera. They watched as she sped out of sight on the path leading towards the bachelor and bachelorette pods.

"I tried to run with her once," Tallah said. "I quickly learned it wasn't my thing, and she is much happier when she gets to have frequent runs."

"Oh yes! I know full well." Koi just laughed. He'd also attempted to run with Vera on more than one occasion. So, he understood exactly what Tallah was talking about. Vera could definitely be militant in her need to run and was often inpatient if she had to slow down or not run as far as she'd desired.

# CHAPTER FIVE

When all three were once again tucked safely inside the house They quickly whipped up a simple meal, mushrooms, freshwater shrimp wrapped in flat bread with tomato and pepper sauce. They saved the conversation for while they ate.

"I was able to take the moral high ground and it was all I could do to not laugh as I left him sitting there. I swear he didn't know what hit him. If he had any inclination that I wasn't Strictly by the book that's all washed away now!" She practically floated on her seat as she told her friends about her meeting at the café.

"Well," said Tallah, "at work today I told my supervisor about my mushroom experiment figured I didn't want to give them a reason to look twice at me. They just wrote it down and said they'd send the information it to L.A.B.S. since technically it's genetic manipulation. I happily agreed but goodness I hope they don't take it. I'd love to see how big it's going to get." Vera had slipped out during the mushroom talk and returned with the box. The lock on the side was five round dowels that could be turned with symbols on them.

"We've tried every possible combination. The only thing that has ever happened is the dowels on the ends will pop up with a small sharp spike." Koi said as he spun one of the dowels before pushing it towards Tallah.

She had been looking at the dowels for five minutes before glancing up. When she looked up from the table, she was annoyed by the fact that both of their faces were glued to her. Wide eyes watched her every movement.

"You two have to get away. I need to focus and you're going to make me nervous." She shooed them on with her hand as she went back to working on the dowels.

Walking into the sitting room they sat on large armchairs facing one another. Vera began to smirk at Koi and got up. He watched her walk towards him slightly confused, partly intrigued by her face. He'd never seen this look in her eye before. She didn't hesitate in completing her plan of action either. She sat down in his lap.

"We don't have to struggle to find alone time to steal a kiss anymore." She said before wrapping her arms around him and kissing him softly, but passionately. It's really surprising that they heard anything outside of each other, but somehow they did.

"Ouch!!" They heard Tallah exclaim from the kitchen. Vera started to get up and check on her, but Koi held her at the waist and instead spoke loudly.

"Little spike get you?" he asked.

Her response was muffled, as if her finger was in her mouth but still understandable. "Yes, good grief that's sharp!"

"Our moms must have really wanted to keep what's in that box hidden to boobie trap the dang thing." He said loudly so she could hear him from the kitchen.

Vera smacked Koi on the arm hard. "Somehooni will hear you! We can't get careless." She growled.

He knew she meant business by the furrowed brow and hard set jaw looking back him.

"You're right. I'm sorry. You're just too good to put down, forgive me?" he asked.

Her kiss of a response was good enough for them both and she laid her head down on his chest and listened to his heart beating. She'd wanted to sit or lay like this for years but had never been able to. This moment was Exhilarating. The next thing the two little lovers knew they were being woke up by a frantic Tallah shaking them and begging them to come to the kitchen.

"Your moms were geniuses! I can't believe I didn't understand this sooner! Come here." She was gushing and practically dragged them into the kitchen.

Rubbing her eyes Vera looked at the clock on the wall and was shocked that it said 3am.

"You haven't slept?" she asked if Tallah.

"Um... no! Puzzle! Mystery! Danger for possibly all Hoonikind! Of course, I haven't slept you twit!!" Tallah responded in a crazed sounding voice.

"Well, I'm awake now, gosh Tallah." She said as her and Koi approached the box.

Tallah quickly apologized but didn't slow down in her explanation of the lock.

"The symbolism on the dowels is genetic sequencing, they have to be dialed in at the same time to form the basic code of what a Hooni is. When that happens both spikes come up, also at the same time. It took me FOREVER to get the connection. But the first set of genetic identification is Hooni plain and simple. The second is more precise. These spikes are hollow! Look for yourself." She handed them a massive magnifying glass and sure enough both spikes had a hole in the center. Koi and Vera were amazed and began telling Tallah that it was amazing she'd figured all that out.

"We'll all go to bed and hopefully tomorrow we can continue on this. It's impressive you've done in a night what we couldn't in years-" Before Vera could finish, Tallah, in her second very unhooni like action of the night, cut Vera's sentence in half and continued talking.

"Nonsense I've already figured out the spikes purpose. It's to take blood from each of your mom's fingers. The lock has some kind of DNA reader they installed inside it so that truly they would be the only ones to open the box. Luckily we happen to have two people in this room who share a similar genetic information of each of the brilliant minds who designed this lock." She inhaled sharply as if all her air had been used in her explanation.

"The only thing I'm unsure of is which spike is for which of you. I need you to look, see if anything is significant that may point to who was supposed to be on which side, I think it has to be simultaneously done."

This luckily was a no brainer. In a single glance Vera knew immediately which dowl held the spike that had belonged to her mother and subsequently to Koi's mother. With the dowels lined up the hues of the ink on one side were all a particular shade of blue that had been Kai's favorite. The other side held a similar color but if you knew the women you knew which shade of blue, they each favored. A single tear made its way down Vera's cheek.

"I know which side belongs to each of us. It's the color difference on the symbols." Vera stated.

Tallah looked at the dowels. "I don't see the difference. Some hues of blues are indistinguishable from other hues to some of us. It's a common genetic thing actually. You'd have gotten your ability to tell the difference in the two from your mother. A third genetic code to the lock. Impressive ladies." It was as if Tallah was talking directly to Koi and Vera's mothers.Tallah told them to each prick their fingers on the spikes and allow the blood to drop inside of it. Just as they went to do it though she stopped them in a panic.

"No! Wait. It's already early in the morning. If we do this who knows what's next, plus I don't want to leave this box unlocked all day while we're at work. No, best that you return it to your hiding place, and we resume this after work again tomorrow."

Vera blinked slowly and in an exaggerated manner while pulling her lips to the center, biting the inside of them. She had literally been trying to say something along the same lines a minute ago, but she knew Tallah was in puzzle mode and driven by excitement. So, she simply said.

"Sounds great. Now BED Everyhooni!" Without formalities the three split and each went to their own beds. Koi had kept his window ajar that morning so sneaking back in was simple and silent. They all slept a deep dreamless sleep. Not that they slept long, 5am came rapidly.

Koi didn't walk with the women, he normally didn't anyway but they'd decided they needed to keep their distance in public just to be safe. Vera and Tallah didn't speak on their walk, other than saying bye as Vera parted ways to go towards the school. Both were just too exhausted.

The school day dragged on. It was a typical day otherwise, her mind kept wondering off to the almost unlocked box hidden in her closet. They were so close to figuring out what Kai and Naandi had been working on. She may find out exactly what her mother gave her life up for. She missed her mother very much. Kai and Naandi lived side by side in the widow pod. They rarely spoke of their husbands. Koi and Vera's dads had both died when they were toddlers. A massive fire had started at one of the farms and everyhooni came to beat back the flames.

Twelve Hooni died when the building they were in collapsed. It was among the largest disasters that had ever happened on Dayak. Despite whatever was currently going on, at least Dayak ran smoothly, and the people were safe and happy. She allowed this fact to fuel her through the rest of her day.

Koi popped into her classroom as usual at the close of the day. "I had a student missing today. I can only assume she was from the hunting and foraging pods. It made me sick to my stomach." His voice cracked while he told her.

Vera didn't know what to say. She put her hands on his shoulders as she passed around behind him. Just touching him made her feel better, she hoped that it had the same benefits for him.

"I have to go to do my gatherings with the rest of my housemates today, Vera. I can't miss it. I'll be noticed. It'll be later before I can come over to work on the box." Koi informed her. She knew there was no way around a houses schedule so there was no point in arguing.

"That's fine we probably should go to the farms to collect the rest of our shares for the week also. Speaking of which, I need to meet Tallah, so she doesn't walk all the way to the crossroads, since the farm is past her building. Wouldn't want her to have to double back." Vera quickly kissed Koi's cheek as she hurried out the door without looking back. Leaving Koi to watch her billowing skirts once again as she zipped down the hallway and out the back door of their school building.

Clothing on Dayak was indeed unique. The Omega team had brought with them knowledge from their day of synthetic material. It was an interesting chemical reaction. It started off as a liquid, once mixed to the correct specifications it was poured into a large rectangular mold. Once it cured it was rolled up as a giant bolt of breathable, flexible fabric. If the fabric was to be worn by someone going into the jungle more of a particular agent was mixed in which made the fabric more durable and harder to tear or puncture. A must have for walking through areas riddled with thorns.

Most Hooni made their own clothing, material was allotted to each hooni yearly, but the fabric lasted years. Any article of clothing that was outgrown or had just finally lost its shape or faded badly was turned into the fabric department at the council building. It could be recycled easily. There was no waste on Dayak. Many styles of clothing existed, however with this type of process for making fabric, there were no patterns that would have been common from woven textile fabric of the past. All clothing on Dayak were solid colors. It lended itself to the unity of hooni kind, in the same way that uniforms bound sport teams of long ago.

Vera made it to the door of the grow rooms where Tallah worked, but before she could reach out to open it a group of garden-based scientists exited.

Tallah was among them. She quickly told her coworkers goodbye and joined Vera.

The walk to the farms was not very far. They had built the greenhouse and grow rooms nearby since the material from one would have to be transferred to the farm at some point anyway. Each gathered a few leafy greens, some carrots and a couple of squash. They liked to coordinate their gatherings sometimes to make dishes that they both liked. Zucchini casserole bread was their favorite, so when the zucchini looked great, they'd both load up on that and forgo the other produce, but today it was all about just getting the job done to get back to the house quickly. Once Tallah had her mindset for a puzzle she rarely thought about anything else. When she brought up her day on the walk home it didn't surprise Vera that Tallah hadn't mentioned it sooner.

"We had two people not show up for work. I found out that they live in the same pod and got into an argument yesterday. The corrections officer came and got them. Took them to the sick bays at the L.A.B.S. and will probably be taking them on to the inmate facilities"

"I'd like to say I'm shocked, but in honesty, I'm almost numb over it." Vera said without looking up.

Tallah kicked a rock down the path and responded, "that's sad, I wish I knew what was going on."

"Soon as Koi gets to the house tonight, we'll go back at it." Vera responded. She and Vera looked up and gave one another reassuring smiles.

The walk home was mostly silent from there. The two simply looked at the beautiful island that they loved. True, they didn't know any other home, but this island and their way of life had felt so perfect last week. It broke both of their hearts a little at the thought that something, or someone was trying to destroy it.

As they got to their home they'd no more than made it into the kitchen when someone knocked on the front door. They assumed it was Koi, Vera ran and grabbed the box placing it on the table and Tallah threw open the door in excitement.

The smile from Tallah's face vanished when she saw a young hunter standing at the door. He was broad shouldered, with a handsome face. His smile almost sparkled and Tallah found herself mute. In an awkward motion she stepped backwards from the door and extended her arm, inadvertently inviting the man inside. It must have been a shock to him as well because he stepped inside like the floor may give way at any moment.

Vera was likewise taken aback by the strangers' presence in the house. She was standing near the sink and swiftly grabbed the dish towel as she walked forwards towards the kitchen table that stood between her and this mystery man. Without a hint of question, she dropped the towel over the box as if she'd done it absentmindedly. Perfectly hiding it.

"Welcome, good day." Vera greeted him formally and with as much respect as she could muster. The man returned the greeting and went on to add that he was

"-Picking up the baskets from your gatherings the day before yesterday. When I came last night after dark, I couldn't find them on your stoop." He glanced from Tallah to Vera but noticeably lingered when he looked at Tallah.

"Oh goodness, I've never forgotten them before I'm so terribly sorry." Tallah said as her voice trailed with her as she ran out of the side door to the spring house to fetch the baskets.

The young man looked directly at Vera and the two grinned knowingly. The blushing across his face had given his thoughts away. When Tallah re-emerged with the baskets in hand she was still apologizing.

"It's okay, it does happen sometimes." He said. His voice had a similar rich deep tone that they'd heard from the hunter in the woods. Tallah was visibly swooning, and Vera couldn't help but come to the rescue.

"You've walked a long way due to our mistake. The least we can do is offer you a cup of tea." Vera told the hunter.

In another quick motion she scooped up the box with the towel on it and left the room. When she came back in Tallah had already started the water to boiling and was talking to the man, who was named Nash.

Vera sat and shared tea but didn't say much. She just watched Nash and Tallah, the kismet between the two was very evident. The conversation was meaningless, but the looks in their faces were priceless. Nash finished his tea, rinsed his cup in the women's sink and in true hooni fashion politely began to excuse himself and bid goodbye. Tallah issued the customary parting responses and the two made their way to the door. Vera was floored that both were going to part ways without any exchange of meeting again. Being the bold and brassy type that she was, Vera couldn't let this muscle bound hooni slip out of their door that easily, seeing as he was perfect for Tallah, and the two so clearly showed a spark for each other.

"Where can we find you at when we come to the gathering stalls? We've been painting the most beautiful flowers from the jungle around there and Tallah had mentioned wanting to explore farther into the interior, but I really have no interest in that, so I'd feel better if she had a guide to ensure her safety."

Nash smiled like a schoolboy, his deep dimples puckering the sides of his face adorably. "I'd be glad to, I'm normally with my brother Bip, he's the main hunter for our pod. Just ask for Nash and Bip and everyhooni will know who you're asking for." He answered before he closed the door and left.

Tallah stood staring at the closed door. Turning and leaning her back against its smooth wood she began to slowly sink down it. Halfway she stopped her descent. She looked like she was sitting on an imaginary chair against the door. When Koi knocked she dreamily let him in.

She wafted into the kitchen. Koi hugged Vera and pointed at Tallah, with a questioning look on his face.

"Is she okay?" he asked.

"Absolutely, her destiny came by and his name is Nash." She smirked while she went to get the box for the second time that night.

"He was kind and intelligent and had dimples for days." She told Koi.

"That's nice." He answered. He was ready to get down to business and couldn't get as excited over an attractive guy as Vera and Tallah obviously were.

# CHAPTER SIX

Tallah wiped the remainder of the giddiness off her face and went to work on the dowels. She reset them in the perfect configuration and 'click', out popped the two spikes in unison.

"It's now or never" Tallah said as she gestured for them to go ahead and prick their fingers.

They moved their fingers over their respective spikes and counted, "one, two, three," pressing their fingers down and then waiting as the droplets of blood were almost sucked into it.

Everyone sat staring at the box. Anxious it wouldn't open and terrified it would. Although the box didn't open immediately, no one moved. Their patience was soon rewarded. A quick burst of air from under the rim of the lid forced it open about two inches.

Vera found both Koi and Tallah looking at her, as a silent vote had been unknowingly taken and she had been chosen to open it. You could have heard a pin drop to the floor as she rolled her eyes and pulled the box towards her. Outwardly she was calm and passive, inside she was on fire, curiosity and anticipation swirled with fear and nervousness. The cocktail was enough to make her want to vomit. She pushed onward anyway and opened the lid. Inside lay two Manila folders. One was marked, *__Lab test__* the other *__Findings of drug trials.__*

"Well, looks like we have some reading to do." Vera informed them.

She split her folder's stack with Tallah and handed the other folder to Koi. They all unanimously moved to the more comfortable chairs in the living room with its soft pillows. As they read on into the night and passed folders back and forth there was never a grand eureka moment. Sure, the data and test and drugs were all a little suspicious and definitely were not being ran by the council, the notes down the side of the margins implied that Lotta was pressuring everyone and being demanding and harsh. Still nothing worth them dying over.

All three discussed what they'd been reading and felt very deflated. They walked back into the kitchen.

"Just because our moms didn't give us answers here didn't mean that there wasn't something going on then, and there definitely is something going on now. So even if we don't have their help, we have to keep going and get to the bottom of this."

They all handed Tallah the folders and she slapped them down into the box. Just before she was about to close the lid she exclaimed. "This is ridiculous, there's no reason to make a box this intricate for some stolen work reports. I just don't get it!"

She slapped the top of the folders that lay inside the box. When she did this a '*hiss*' could be heard by everyone in the room. They all looked around and cross checked each other's faces to verify they'd all heard the same noise and then looked at the box beneath Tallah's hand.

She slowly lifted her hand, where the two folders no longer lay flat against the bottom of the box but were raised up ever so slightly. Quickly yet carefully she removed the folders and there was no doubt. This box indeed had a false bottom. She touched it but in no way could she get her fingers under it to lift it up.

Koi ran to the silverware drawer and got a kitchen knife. The two women wrapped their arms around each other and held their breath. Carefully he slid the knife under and lifted the hatch open. There in the hidden chamber laid a thin folder, not very different from the two they'd found above. On the cover in Vera's mother's distinct handwriting, they saw their names,

***Vera & Koi***.

Vera momentarily forgot how to Breathe, until her body forced her to take a shaky breath inward. She stood fixed to the spot. Once they opened this folder there would be no unseeing it, they couldn't unlearn what they were about to find out.

Koi ran his fingers across their names on the folder as if to second that he was experiencing a similar feeling that Vera was. Tallah had allowed herself to sink into a chair. This moment held an unexpected weight that laid heavily on all their shoulders.

Tallah knew it was too much for her friends, so for the first time in her life she was bold. Picking up the folder and laying in front of her. It was like jumping into cold water. No amount of preparation helps, you just have to hold your nose and jump. So that's what she did, opening the folder she cleared her throat and began to read aloud.

Dear Koi & Vera

We're writing this letter to explain something horrible. If you've found this, then we believe you're aware something is not right on Dayak and you're searching for answers. Sadly, we feel we may not be around when you begin to question the world. We're torn between wanting to hide this well and fearing we're going to hide it so well you two can't find it.

As you know we worked for L.A.B.S.. What you may not know is exactly what we did. We were Geneticist. Normally that just entailed making sure our food sources were resistant to pest and that any illness among the hooni could be squashed before it became a problem.

However, we stumbled upon something when you two were very small. Naandi figured it out first actually, but with her being my best friend she told me immediately. We trusted each other, you two must do the same.

The more test we ran trying to alter genetic sequencing on hooni to make them be able to fight this new illness that came from the monkeys, the more we realized that the monkeys were a scape goat, we were working on a way to alter hooni genetics in general. To alter us, not for an illness prevention but for something far more sinister.

Okay, we're going to try and be as factual as possible and not long winded. Here's the story, from the start.

When the Omega team set sail for Dayak, they told the humans that they were being given an injection to safeguard against viruses, to keep Dayak safe. It was a lie from the beginning. The ten humans who made the core of the Omega team had figured out how to alter humans genetically, change their brain's biochemistry. The injections made humans lose their desire to be assertive and aggressive in any capacity. While that may not seem like a big deal, it was. Because it did more than just that. It prohibits the alpha traits that all animals have. It makes everyone subservient. We don't believe the Omega team intended to harm anyone, they simply didn't want the war and terror that was taking over their world to be brought into the utopia they were trying to create. The injections didn't create mindless slaves, they wanted peace, not zombies. However now that the spirit and will of the humans had been broken, the core team established rules and customs that would enforce this placid attitude. It had other concerns for the core team. Remember, they're intentions were genuinely good, they didn't want harm to come to Dayak. That's why they set up the council and the rules. They thought as long as it was ran in kindness it would always be okay.... nothing altered can ever truly be okay.

You know we're a different species from that of our human ancestors, what you don't know is, those injections started the changes that led to us being so different. It was what started the evolutionary ball rolling so to speak. It's our evolution that's actually being the downfall to the injection's effectiveness now though.

You see, what Naandi figured out, is that around a hundred years ago, less than five percent of children ever had disciplinary issues. Now, that number is climbing rapidly.

All hooni babies are given the omega injections at birth. Always have. That used to be enough until it wasn't. That's when the highest member of L.A.B.S. instituted the three strikes for children.

Our elder high table at the council aren't even aware of this. They think they run Dayak, but the L.A.B.S. do. It's always been a shell game.

The bland meals to symbolize that we miss out on the joys of Dayak when we fail to be good hooni, are laced with more of the chemicals from the injections. Obviously when a child is taken for their next infraction, the injections are heavier doses of the same stuff.

When an adult gets out of line and is taken to the corrections facility, you can probably guess by now it's more biochemistry altering work being done and NOT rehabilitation therapy!

As I mentioned before, our very evolution is at play here. Simply put, we've changed genetically so much that the injections are having less and less effectiveness on us.

In a sense we're waking up and the L.A.B.S. are having a harder time controlling us.

Now, at first, we struggled with this information. At its core, it's good. Our society runs smoothly, and people are healthy, safe, and happy as a whole. The next bit of information is why we chose to take action.

The heads of L.A.B.S., Lotta, has went too far. She thinks she's more intelligent than any hooni has ever been. She thinks she's entitled to more than her shares.

She's plotting something, although we're not sure what. Her father and grandfather before her ran the Genetic rooms. They had a sense of superiority that had never been seen before. They'd began something among their family. Naandi and I didn't understand that, but we had to figure out how to keep our kids from getting the injections. Koi did have his first ones, but we worked hard to keep you from having any further ones. Vera when you were born You were dead. The Nanny laid you in my arms and as I wept you took a breath. In all the confusion and joy the very new, young nanny helping me with you forgot to give you the injection. I of course didn't want to let you go so I kept my mouth shut. You, Vera are the first Hooni that's 100% unvaccinated, to our knowledge. Lotta is power hungry. She's doing very unethical test to try and retain that power. I wish we had more information for you. We do know, that for some reason, the Hooni in the hunter gatherer pods are the most resistant to the injections. They're also an annoyance to Lotta and we think she both fears and targets them. At this time, it's all we know. Should we learn more, we'll put it in here. If not, please know that you're loved, trust your instincts.

Love, Kai & Naandi"

It was almost too much; tears stung her eyes and she was forced to cover her mouth with her hand as this moment came crashing down on her. Tallah ran her hands around the bottom of the false bottom. This was indeed the actual bottom of the box. No further information could be found within it. She placed the papers back inside the box as they'd originally been. Closed the secret false bottom, placed the other folders in the main part of the box and clicked the lid closed. Lastly, she spun the dowels resetting them to a locked position.

She silently rose from the table and gave Vera a minute to be alone with Koi. Sitting in the living room the information she'd read kept washing over her like waves. Her whole life she'd been a puppet. Her servitude for the greater good like an ant for the colony. She had once felt like she was part of something big and important. Now she simply felt small and empty.

Koi and Vera came into the living room where Tallah sat. They stared at her and worried that this all may be too much to handle. Vera went and knelt down in front of Tallah. She was ready to do anything from comfort her to hold her down to keep her from running away.

Tallah snapped her tear-stained face up. Looking into Vera's eyes she flatly said,

"I, in no way, am letting Lorn, his mother, or anyhooni ruin our world. I know I said I was all in before... but now I'm determined to fix this giant mess and I'm not giving up or backing down one drop."

Vera stumbled backwards from her crouched position, landing firmly on her bottom with her feet splayed out in front of her. The smile that spread over her face quickly turned into laughter. That laughter was quickly spread to the other two occupants of the room. They, knew they had a long way to go, but at least now they knew which direction to go in.

"Thanks mom." Vera whispered as she climbed into bed that night.

The next day at school everything seemed lighter for Vera. Like the mystery had been a burden she'd carried so long that she had become habituated to it. Now that it was no longer hanging on her like a wet blanket, she felt renewed. She was different, and it was a good thing.
Her mother hadn't just died aimlessly. She was KILLED... and now she knew why. Her mother had given her life trying to save her, and all Hooni kind. Picking up this torch felt like Honor inside her. She would finish what her mother started; she would save Dayak. She still hadn't figured out how, but she

was determined. A determined spirit, armed with courage and intelligence could prevail against anything... she hoped.

# CHAPTER SEVEN

At lunch she and Koi stood against the far wall like always watching the room. The children were calmly eating their lunch, when Vera saw a facial expression flash across the room that read loud and clear of anger.

She walked immediately towards the young girl. The girl was very pretty, her hair was in near perfect dreadlocks. Uniformed in shape with a reddish-brown color and beautiful white wooden beads on some of the strands. She was very thin, willowy to be more precise. Her eyebrows were furrowed at the girl across the table who was staring back at her with an equally angry face. She too was just as wispy thin as the first girl. Her hair was pulled tight and smooth into a set of braids that Zigzagged across her head in an intricate pattern, her hair had the same white beads in it.

Vera called them both by name and asked them if they'd be so willing to come help her with something. Both girls politely nodded and rose from the table. Once she had them in her classroom, she turned her attention to the real reason they'd been plucked from the cafeteria.

"I saw the anger in your faces from across the room." Vera told them.

She looked from one girls face to the other one. As she did so she was struck with how similar they looked. They were almost doubles of each other. She guessed they must be sisters. She knew she couldn't ask though.

They both began to sob softly and then they started begging.

"Please don't call the L.A.B.S. mama warned us already. We don't want to be taken like Deevid. There will be no one left to help mama with the work and the babies." The almost cried.

Vera struggled for a second to keep up. "Wait are you Deevids older sisters?" She asked.

"Yes ma'am." They both looked absolutely panic stricken.

"Spill it, what's really going on." She asked.

One sister started talking and quickly the other grabbed her hand and squeezed it several times. Almost as if pumping out a code telling her to stop.

"Reelah, don't." She finally said when she realized her sister wasn't going to stop talking."

Reelah shushed her sister and pressed on, "No Tayah, we need help. The L.A.B.S. haven't brought Deevid back, Papa has been on an extended hunt in the jungle for a month, and mama has the twins too. I'm terrified. Please don't tell that we were angry."

Vera exhaled loudly and laid her head down on her desk with an audible 'thunk'

She began talking before picking her head up. Giving her voice a muffled echoing sound for the first few words of her sentence.

"I won't tell on two conditions. 1. You don't tell anyone I saw you being angry. As far as anyone needs to know I genuinely needed your help in here. 2. Obviously the fact that I am asking about your mother violates a few Hooni codes but here's the big one, don't tell that either because we all three will be in hot water up to our necks. Then who will help your mom? I assume I can find her at the gathering pods?"

Both girls nodded and were dismissed.

By the time she'd made it back to the cafeteria with both girls her lunch shift was over.

As she passed by Koi, she told him. "We're going to the gathering pods today after work. I have something interesting to check into."

Vera checked the clock on the wall continuously that day. She'd have sworn an hour should have passed but would groan when she realized it was only ten minutes or so.

Finally, the hour to dismiss the students came!

"Okay kids, have a good day. See you tomorrow." She said.

As the children filed out, she was straightening desk behind them. When she reached the door, she stood holding it open for the last student to exit.

"Goodbye Karft, your drawing was excellent today. You should enter it in the art contest for Hoonie day." She said as the little guy went past her.

He always had his pockets untucked and was mostly unorganized in every other way. His face lit up and he was obviously overjoyed at finally doing something well. Vera was elated to be able to dote on Karft, she always tried to find strong suits in each of her students to make them feel empowered. Until today she'd came up short with this young man.

When she passed the door to Koi's classroom, she stuck her hand inside and rapidly tapped on the open door. She barely paused to do so and kept walking. Koi realized that he'd be left if he didn't move it. So, like the smart hooniman he was, he immediately got up and followed Vera. It took him several quick steps but before they reached the door at the back of the hallway, and he'd caught up to her.

"For someone with such short legs you sure move fast!" He panted.

She chuckled before she filled him in on what they were rushing of to do. The hair on the back of his neck stood up when she told him that Deevid hadn't yet been returned. Kids were never gone to the L.A.B.S. More than a few hours, let alone overnight.

When they neared the crossroads, they could see Tallah sitting on the bench just past it. Her head was buried in a giant book. As they got closer it was obvious that she wasn't going to look up. Keeping up with her hasty behavior Vera thumped the backside of the book hard when they got to her. Koi slowed to stop but Vera kept going.

Tallah raised her head and exclaimed, "you're early, hey wait where are you going?"

Koi picked up Tallah's bag and told her to come on. "Vera's gonna leave us I do believe."

When they were all walking three abreast on the path Koi pointed out, "Vera, you have to slow down! I can't keep up without running."

Vera didn't acknowledge him and began to tell Tallah where they were going and why. Koi snapped and interrupted her, taking both women by surprise.

"VERA! Slow down now! You're going to draw attention to us." He groaned.

She stopped walking instantly. "You're right. I'm sorry. I'm just overwhelmed."

Koi and Tallah were both nearly panting as they rested their hands on their knees.

"It's okay, we just have to stay steady and get to the bottom of this, otherwise we'll be joining Deevid, or be the recipients of a triple funeral." He said.

She knew he was right. She smoothed her skirt with her hands and took a big inhale before starting the trek off again, this time at a much more normal pace.

"What are you going to do anyway Vera?" Tallah asked. "You can't just walk up and tell the woman, what's going on. Everything you're doing, not to mention everything you did to lead up to this is against hooni ways and violates several of your teacher codes of ethics."

Vera grumbled, sounding like she was speaking words without moving her mouth bobbing her head back forth as she did so. It looked like she was arguing with herself. Had the situation been different it could have been slightly comical.

"Ugh I don't really know. I tried to pre plan this conversation out all day. It's impossible though, so I'm just gonna wing it." Vera answered after she stopped grunting to herself.

Up ahead the gathering stalls came into view. The sound of pleasant conversations and the crinkles of things being wrapped up in banana leaves filled the space as they closed in.

Vera saw two hunters standing behind the stall tables, they were having what appeared to be a much-needed drink of water. They were covered in sweat. The smaller of the two was Nash, the larger one was the same man they'd seen Lorn threatening the other day.

Vera made a polite greeting to the lady at the stall's helm and then asked her if she could get Nash to come over.

"We're friends." She added quickly as the lady scrutinized her with a tilt of the head.

"I'm his sister Kajaah." She finally said with a slight smile. She leaned around to look behind Vera. "You must be Tallah, Nash described you so well it's painted a visual picture of you for me, nice to meet you all." With that she turned and went to get Nash, leaving Tallah blushing.

Tallah found something hidden inside of her when Nash walked over, a tiny seed of courage that the secrets in the locked box had fueled. She stepped forward and spoke to Nash without hesitation.

"I'm so glad to see you, I do apologize for interrupting your work, is that your brother Bip?" she asked as she motioned towards the giant Mountain sized Hooni that lingered by the water bucket where Nash had left him.

The smile on Nash's face was perfect, his dimples were only outshined by the sparkle in his eye as he gazed into Tallah's mousy little face.

"Yes, it is." He nodded while answering her. "I will be happy to take you to see the flowers you wanted, but first may we stop by the riverbank, I need desperately to wash my face. Today, the jungle won, and I am ever the mess for it." Foragers and hunters had lengthy poetic sentences that differed ever so slightly from most other Hooni.

"Of course, but I need another favor, if it isn't too rude of me to ask, Vera is looking for a woman, she has a son, named Deevid. Do you know where she can be found?" Tallah asked without one faltered note in her voice.

His eyes grew large, and he leaned in towards them so that only the three could hear what he was saying, "it's very strange what is happening. Please tell me you do not bring bad news from the L.A.B.S.."

Vera, while happy that Tallah was taking charge and feeling so emboldened felt the need to grab the conversation before it got away from them.

"No, we don't work with the L.A.B.S., I'm actually head teacher and Deevid is in my class. I'm concerned by his absence, and I had some clues that pointed to him living in the gathering Pods. Please don't think badly of me for coming to call on his mother. I know it's very unorthodox, but my worry has superseded the need to follow protocol in this situation." She calmly stated.

Nash straightened himself back upright and began pointing his first two fingers at Vera and shaking his hand slightly up and down, all three held their breath for a moment worried they were about to be scolded when he chuckled and said,

"I knew I liked you two! You're iconoclast at heart." He softly chuckled.

Iconoclast was akin to a vulgar word among the Hooni. Vera had encountered it in a book about ancient humans her mother had left open when she was small. Kai found her with her dolls using the words iconoclast and rebel freely in her imaginary world of play. Never had her mother been angrier.

She'd been told that any word linked to a rebellion was forbidden among their kind. That it sewed hate and distrust. 'Dayak is perfect, and we must never undermine its values.' She'd said.

"I haven't met you." Nash said as he introduced himself to Koi.

The two exchanged normal civil greeting before Nash turned to lead them away down a footpath behind the gathering stalls. None of them had ever been this way. Hunter and gathers rarely had outside visitors. Tallah walked beside Nash and made small talk as Koi pulled up level with Vera.

"Not to sound ignorant, but what Does iconoclast mean?" he asked.

Vera chuckled and gave him a quick answer "it means a person who attacks cherished beliefs or an institution."

"That's us then!" He said in a matter-of-fact kind of way.

The first pod came into view. The houses were all older in appearance, and sported vines and flowers clinging to them. Moss covered roofs and low limbs with hanging foliage gave them a hidden cozy feeling. Never had Vera been so comfortable anywhere. At the same time though, she wondered how the housing department allowed these homes to differ so from the standard of Hooni houses.

Passing the turn to the first pod, they continued into the jungle until three more pod paths had been passed. On the tenth pod entrance they turned and began walking the circle to one of the houses at the backside of the pod. There they found a house similar to the others they'd passed. Run down, but charming. Nash went to the side of the house and let himself into the adjoining backyard that the pod shared.

"Nash, shouldn't we knock at the front first?" Tallah asked. She was obviously uneasy by this point. Her confidence had waned some.

"Normally yes, but I live in this pod, so it is my backyard also." He kept walking as he spoke.

A branch of beautiful purple flowers obscured their approach. Nash lifted it up and motioned for the three following him to go on under and ahead of him. They found themself in a yard with children running everywhere. At least a dozen were playing tag. Several older children were standing at a large soup pot hanging over an open fire. Yet more still were hanging laundry on a long line that stretched from the corner of one house to another.

Vera felt a lump in her throat. The fact that she had no clue how to proceed with this investigation hit her all at once. She was so overwhelmed she wanted to turn and run away. She pushed that feeling down deep into her. Following Nash to the house at the far side of the yard.

A woman was sitting with two babies asleep in a woven basket at her feet and sewing up a hole in a pair of heavy work gloves, obviously belonging to her husband.

"Rhoan, these hooni need to talk to you. This one is Deevid's teacher." He said while he pointed, again with two fingers, towards Vera.

The woman issued all the normal formalities. When she attempted to stand to be polite Vera insisted, she stay seated. "I don't need the pomp and ceremony Rhoan, may My friend Koi and I sit and join you?" Nash began talking, almost as if he wanted to interject himself into this situation and stay as a self-appointed chaperone or mediator. Rhoan quickly stopped him by holding up her hand,

"Nash I'm fine. If Vera and her friends could drag themselves all the way out here and violate dozens of hooni rules, not to mention put her position as council member and her job in jeopardy..." she paused before finishing "I'm sure I can trust them with anything I may say that is itself a little unhooni'. Take Tallah and get to know her better."

She dismissed Nash and Tallah with a sweep of hand. Vera couldn't suppress a smile, wondering how many hooni Nash had talked to about the pretty girl who'd so quickly stolen his heart.

Tallah looked from Vera's face to Rhoans' and when Vera nodded in agreement she turned and took Nash by the hand. The two disappeared behind the hanging laundry line and continued away from the pods towards the river beyond.

# CHAPTER EIGHT

Rhoan picked up the conversation with a force that made the hair on the back Vera and Koi's neck tingle. She was loose lipped and spoke open and flippedly with an unapologetic distain for the L.A.B.S.

"I know you've came about my boy. The L.A.B.S. won't bring him home. I'm afraid he's dead and no one will tell me. They took my brother off to the correctional facility several months ago for arguing with that 'Lorn' fellow near the gathering stall square. He should have been there one week for his punishment and behavior therapy. If you ask me something fishy is going on.

Nash, Bip and my husband Brev have doubled their workloads all because of Lorn's needs. It isn't Hooni of me to tattle, but it's also not hooni of Lorn to come here and demand so much." She said then fixed her gaze far away. Like her mind had so much more to say than her body would allow.

As if walking on a slippery surface Vera began to slowly and carefully edge around the topic on her mind.

"Yes, I am in fact very concerned about Deevid, but it's more so of what the L.A.B.S. have to do with him and really the rest of our lives that I'm wanting to speak to you about. This is, as you said unhooni and terribly uncomfortable for me speak about. I do however think we're on a similar page with our thinking and can trust one another though." Vera said in a calm, low voice, careful to not wake the Babies nor draw attention from anyone else.

"You say your husband and others are overworked. Do you know how, or for what?"

The lady turned her eyes back towards Vera without moving her head. Giving her a knowing quality.

"I do indeed. Lorn wants monkeys for testing on. Our men can't stop their hunting and fishing, or Dayak will starve, yet these monkey trapping trips are very difficult and laborious, so they are working themselves to death. I was told that there's a sickness caused by the monkeys that the labs are trying to stop.

"In the beginning when my father would go on monkey excursions, not as often as now mind you, but when he'd go, my mother was worried that he or us kids would catch whatever illness it was. Now I don't worry about that. These monkeys are healthy. If they weren't they'd be easier to catch. All these years and all these hundreds of monkeys for the L.A.B.S. means only one thing, the monkeys are a cover for something. They'd have cured the illness by now, and we'd have seen sick monkeys but as I've said we have NOT ever seen such. Not to mention what Hooni were ever sick from monkeys in the first place? The only ones who came in contact with the blasted things would have been people from our pods and we never saw anyone sick, EVER."

Vera and Koi exchanged worried glances. She was walking a tightrope between finding out as much as she could from this new source without Divulging to much from her side. She knew this woman was intuitive and could probably smell a fabrication before it could cross her Tongue anyway. So, she just started talking, rebellions have to have a starting point. This is as good as anywhere she figured. Who better to trust than an enemy of your enemy? With caution she began.

"I agree with you. The monkey excursions are not what they seem. I overheard Lorn talking very nastily to Bip about getting monkeys the other day. It made me sick inside. When Deevid didn't return, that sick feeling settled into my bones, and I can't shake it. Coming here, I'm shocked. Your homes are beautiful, but they seem forgotten.

"Your pods don't seem the same as the rest of Dayak. How can we be all the same if I can easily see inequality? The Dayak I love and hold pride for, isn't represented here. I am on the council; I am in a Precarious situation. I want to get to the bottom of this. I want to figure out how to help. How to fix an obviously broken Dayak. The trouble is that I must convince people to fix something that they don't know is broken. I'm gathering all the information I can in order to help.

"I want to make sure that when I do open my mouth, and become UnHooni at a council meeting that I have all the information I need, and that I also don't leave anyhooni hurt in my wake. If I make anything worse for you or anyhooni in order to help, then I've failed. I promise to protect you, and yours. I hope I can find the same loyalty in you."

Rhoan sat back deeply into her chair. "You're a different kind of Hooni aren't you?" She obviously used this as a statement and not a question because she continued talking. "If you're set to help us and hopefully find my Deevid, I'll help and protect you at any cost. Our homes got left out of the upgrades about four generations ago. When Lorn's great great whatever decided that the hunter gathers needed to be allowed to live 'in ways that reflect their environment.'

"What my papa said was it was his weaseling way to allocate more work towards the housings pods where he and his children would be living. The housing department slowly pulled away from us. We don't even get moved around to different pods by them much, if ever anymore. Nash still lives with his mother, to help her since his father died and she's old.

"When we have someone who didn't grow up in our pods that test or marry in, they get put in the pods closer to stalls. They're newer and nicer. I suppose it's a way to ease them into being here. We also experience other things that seem to slight us, but like all Dayak life, we're to be silent and keep working for the greater good."

The babies began to stir in their basket. "These two haven't been to the nanny pods in two weeks. I've not been able to get there and still tend to the foraging in my husband's absence. I got a visit from one of the young nannies yesterday. Saying if I failed to resume sending them soon, I'd be reported.

Tomorrow I had planned to send them with my older daughters to drop at the nanny pods for me before school. It's going to be a long trek in the dark. Nash has forbidden me from doing so.

"He says it's too dangerous lately to send out children at dark, he wouldn't go into any more detail as to why now is more dangerous than normal. He's volunteered to take them each morning. I don't know what I'd do without that young man. Your Tallah had better be equally wonderful."

Vera leaned over and picked up one of the now fully awake babies. The soft hair on its head was poofed up adorably. Rhoan held the other one. Looking at these babies made Vera even more aware that she had to uncover the full extent of whatever Lorn was doing as quickly as possible.

"She is, Tallah is intelligent, beautiful, and kindhearted." Vera said as she handed the second baby to Rhoan. Squeals of delight erupted across the pod yard. They looked up to see Tallah and Nash playing tag with the kids. So many emotions filled her heart. Despite all the bad, she was happy to see Tallah having fun.

They all slept hard that night. They'd had so many long nights and had been running on adrenaline for days that when the moon rose in the sky, they needed no excuse to go to bed. The women had their meal alone where Vera and Tallah exchanged the minutes of their visits with Nash and Rhoan. Koi went straight to his pod after they left the gathering areas. It was nice for the girls to be alone again. The workday for all three the next day was also uneventful.

When Vera stepped out from the school and collected Tallah the two walked to the café for a much-needed cup of coffee. The work and school schedule on Dayak was six days long. Everyone had one day a week off their main jobs to participate in community service. Tallah and Vera were scheduled to help with the community's pollination garden the next day. Koi was set to path maintaining which is what most young men did. Weeding and packing places that rain had disturbed.

Having their coffee felt very normal. Neither of them mentioned their covert knowledge or self-appointed mission. They could have almost forgot that it existed. Until lady Vazeet pulled the empty chair from the table and sat with them. smoothly she sipped her coffee and looked at the two young women as if she'd not just plopped herself uninvited into their midst.

"I couldn't believe my eyes when I looked up from my sisters window yesterday and saw you two talking to Rhoan." Vazeet said without any formalities.

She just left the sentence floating in the air like an Odor lingering long after the source was gone. Neither woman knew exactly how to handle it. Instead, they all sat silently staring at each other.

"I don't know what you're up to girls, but I'd advise you be cautious." Laying another open-ended statement onto the table.

This time Vera picked it up. "Tallah is basically courting a hunter from that pod. We didn't know you were there. I stayed and talked to Rhoan, who Nash introduced us to, while Tallah and he went for a walk. It was my first time in that area, and I loved it." She smiled as a finale attempt to sell her story.

Luckily it seemed to be enough to satisfy the old woman. She sipped at her coffee and creating an awkward silence at the table. Upon setting her cup down she leaned in towards them. "Council meeting is in two days, I'm elated to find a kindred spirit in you Vera. I must warn you again, be cautious.. extremely cautious. If I saw you, others may have too. While most Hooni in that area are a bit of a fringe group and wouldn't report things since they don't notice small oddities, but others, especially those in the first several pods are much stricter. Ever since Lorn and Lotta's ancestor got rejected by a beautiful woman from my pod, we were set aside and scrutinized. There's a little more secret information for you. I can only hope that you share your secret information with me too soon."

Vera could feel her insides shaking. The magnitude of the situation seemed to keep growing.

"I do have something concerning." Vera confessed. "Lorn asked me to coffee this week. I had assumed it was a date attempt until he brought up council matters. He wanted me to not only vote against councilman Eens' proposal to evict the troublemakers from Dayak, but turn them over to the L.A.B.S."

Vazeet nodded and her eyes twinkled eerily. "Same here, minus the date aspect. He came by my home with cut flowers and proposed the same thing to me. He wasn't happy with my answer, what was your response to him, pray tell?" she asked.

Still cautious not to reveal more than needed to satisfy Lady Vazeets' curiosity. "I told him it was shameful for him to discuss such matters in private."

Lady Vazeet laughed one loud chortled sound and lightly sapped the table.

"Good girl, I'm so proud to have you as my successor as head teacher. I'm going to be keeping an eye on you. We may become very good friends. See you at the meeting day after tomorrow. Oh, and Tallah, nice to meet you. I've known Nash since he was born. There's no better Hooni, although your Koi is lovely too." She said with a wink at Vera as she got up and left the two watching her walk calmly out of the café and down the path leading toward the pods where the head senior council members lived.

Vera scoffed and turned to Tallah, "How the mess did that old Hooni know I was with Koi?"

"No clue, but she's not simply a Conscientious bystander. It sounds like she doesn't like Lorn, or his whole lineage" Tallah replied.

"Not sure if I have a new friend in a high place, or a supervisor I have to watch out for." Vera said as she finished her cup of coffee.

They walked home laughing and chatting about the upcoming Hooni day. They'd decided that being sullen or having any air of mystery would be suspicious. If Lady Vazeet had done anything, she'd proven that others are observing them even if they don't know it.

Vera woke before the sun the next morning. She set out to run and have a moment to herself before spending the day tending to the large pollination garden. There were dozens of pollination gardens on Dayak but this one was nearest to the farm and greenhouses that Tallah worked in. It had many beehive boxes and a few fields of flowers and clovers. Beauty had been part of the design and not just function. Nevertheless, work was work no matter how sweet smelling it was.

Leaving her porch at a fast walk quickly turned into a heart pumping sprint. Before she knew it, she could feel her cheeks bouncing rapidly on her face, as her feet rose and fell. She ran until she could smell the salty air wafting in off the ocean. Normally she'd head back at this point on the path. Today however she pressed onward. She ran until the waves lapped over her feet. Standing in the brilliant ocean she looked out towards the horizon line. It was comforting to be reminded of how small she was sometimes.

"At least the whole world isn't dependent upon me." She said to herself. But no sooner than this left her lips could she hear her mother's response to her statement in her mind. 'No, but Vera your whole world is depending on you. Save Dayak.'

With the words 'save Dayak' echoing in her head she ran as fast and as hard as she could backwards her pod. To dress in her heavy work clothes and go play typical Hooni civil servant.

While working Tallah and Vera had split up. Tallah was point hooni for this job detail. Her extensive knowledge of plants meant anytime a question needed answering she was the gal to ask.

Vera had become increasingly uncomfortable when Lorn and his little sister, Phi entered the garden. Vera had never liked Phi anyway, but now her nosy bossy nature seemed more pronounced. Maybe it was just the fact that Vera was on high alert, and now knew Lorn's whole family was doing something that could be the downfall of the whole island.

The workday was so nearly over that Vera let her guard down and moved to an untidy patch where a group of young women were smiling as they worked. Some of them were adorned with body art which was a clear indication of the gathering pods. She wanted to distract herself from the worry over Lorn and Phi and just enjoy the remainder of the day.

She politely introduced herself to the girls around her and began pulling weeds around the tightly packed flowers. Suddenly the girl to her right, with a halo of coily reddish tinted hair dropped a handful of weeds and screamed loudly.

Everyhooni around her immediately stopped what they were doing to come to her aid. "There was a bee inside the clump of weeds. I shoved the stinger right into my hand when I grabbed it. Oh that smarts!" She exclaimed loudly once again.

One of the other ladies with the delicate patterns across their face shushed her and patted her back in a more urgent manner than a comforting one. Making Vera look up and around them.
Lorn was making a quick approach towards them.

"Oh That looks painful. Come on dear." He said as he took the unafflicted hand to lead the young woman with him. She mindlessly obeyed and started away with him.The gatherer hooni that had stood between Vera and the injured girl made a small whimpering sound that could just barely be heard by Vera. It was enough to set Vera into action.

"Wait Lorn." Vera snapped as she stepped forward and placed her hand on the girl's shoulder stopping her from walking.

"Where are you taking her?" She asked.

Lorn looked as if he'd been gob smacked. Clearly, he'd never been challenged in his authority before. "To the L.A.B.S. medic wing. I have a nice salve to make it not swell or hurt anymore."

He attempted to lead the young woman away again when Tallah turned up, drawn over by the commotion. Vera caught her eye and with one alarmed look she had Tallah on board with the mission at hand.

"Good grief Lorn, this doesn't require a trip anywhere. You'd take my workers for a splinter wouldn't you. Vera, go put some honey and wax on this sting and wrap it." She said and dismissed the two women with a wave of her hand.

She then raised her voice so that the whole area could hear her. "We only have one day a week to tend this important garden, I can't spare workers to injury. Everyhooni MUST wear their gloves at all times."

She smiled at Lorn as she passed him. She was completely petrified inside but from the outside she appeared stoic and ever in charge. When she passed Phi, she flashed another smile her way. The two had made the whole event seem tiny and meaningless.

When they waited in line for the rain barrels to wash their hands before leaving Vera was at the end of the last barrel with Tallah laughing and talking softly. Lorn walked up behind them and grabbed them both from the back of their arm right above the elbow. His face was smiling and to any who would have glanced their way he looked like he was happy and having a friendly moment with them. His voice and pinching grip however made them know there was nothing pleasant about this moment.

"Don't ever talk to me like that again. You're lucky I don't report you. You two need to remember your place or I'll make sure you don't have a place to forget. I'll put an end to you..." The hiss in their ears reminding them of the way he'd sounded when he spoke to Bip in the jungle.

Vera jerked her arm hard and cut him off mid-sentence, hitting his hand off Tallah at the same time.

"Don't threaten me, I'm not a hooni you're going to run over that easily." She said taking Tallah by the hand and leaving that washing up line and getting into another shorter one.

"Vera you shouldn't have said that." Tallah said in a shaky voice as she looked back at Lorn who was having a hard time hiding his indignation and anger.

Vera forced herself to stop looking at Lorn and said, "No Tallah. The war has begun. This is only the start. I'm sorry I got you into this, but there's no one I'd rather have in my corner. The whole world is depending on us. We WILL save Dayak."

# CHAPTER NINE

Dinner was almost finished when Koi let himself in. "Well, some of the guys in my pod asked me a million questions last night as to why I've been absent from so many dinners." He said as he sauntered over to the stove where Vera was stirring the large pot. "I brought this guy with me that I found while fixing roads to divert attention from me leaving alone nightly."

Nash took this as his cue to enter the room. Eliciting a squeal from Tallah as she jumped up from where she was cutting leafy greens at the table to be swept into a quick hug by Nash.

Vera was filled with confidence after her first real confrontation at the garden. She grabbed Koi and hugged him tightly. Then surprised the whole room by kissing him passionately right beside the stew pot!

"Not that I'm complaining, but what prompted that?" he asked while blinking dreamily.

Vera pointed the soup spoon towards him and said, "life is unpredictable, that's what! Lorn has lit a fire under me today and the intense anger boiling under my skin has unleashed a whole gambit of emotional awakenings. One of which is my refusal to be anything other than myself. Short of landing in the correctional center I'm about to shake up the world! Tallah, please tell them both, Nash welcome to the revolution, you're in it now whether you wanted to be or not!"

Tallah decided to take charge of this conversation since Vera was apparently to riled up to be much help. Telling the two men about Lorn was done with much care. She went slowly and meticulously. Careful to not leave anything out. When she'd finished Nash was clearly red faced and his hands were squeezed into a tight fist. Koi held his head in his hands.

"Well, say something." Tallah finally said after a few tense moments had passed.

Koi's muffled voice rose up from his hands while his face still laid in his palms. "This is really happening."

"I'll rip him limb from limb." Was Nash's Answer.

Vera looked into Nash's blue eyes. "You have aggressive tendencies?!" She said in a questioning tone.

Everyone turned their attention to Nash

"Yes, when somehooni hurts a hooni I care for of course I do. My mother warned me that this emotion isn't felt by many, but that hunters commonly have it, but I figured since you had a fight with Lorn, maybe mom was wrong." He answered still visibly upset.

All three shook their head 'no' at Nash. Vera decided to continue and give him a bit of an education as to what was happening.

"... and that is why we believe that Lorn wants you and Bip to bring him monkeys. He's lost control over Hoonikind and is actively testing new ways to manipulate the biochemical aspects of the brain. We also think he's attempting to do more than just keep us obedient. He's getting greedy and dangerous there's a group of Hooni who aren't responding at all to the normal protocol at the correctional center.

"Tomorrow's council meeting will hold a vote as to what to do with them. There's been two proposals, one at the last meeting, was councilman Een who wants to set them out in a boat for the mainland. Evict them from Dayak forever. Then the second plan, which Lorn is 'secretly' passing around to try and get support for, that they be completely given over to the L.A.B.S. for testing and study."

Vera paused a few minutes in order to gather herself but before she could continue Nash began talking.

"Firstly, thank you for trusting me. I know that wasn't easy. Growing up in the gathering, fishing, and hunting pods I've been made very aware of what it means to be cautious and secretive. I pledge my loyalty to this and promise, solemnly that I will fearlessly help in any way I can. There's been talk between my family as to what Lorn is doing with the monkeys. Don't worry I won't tell them what you've said.

"Lorn has never used any hunters outside of our pod. He's short tempered and threatening us by saying he can take our kids if we don't comply. My brother and I have been talking about running to the jungle with the families in our pod for safety. Lorn is just continuously getting more demanding and less flexible. He's really worrisome to Bip. Our fear is that he'll do something horrific to another pod in retaliation if we run away."

Vera felt peace and hope wash over her. It seemed like all the pieces of this impossible puzzle were finally all on the table. The only thing left to do now was to put it together.

Standing up she clapped Nash on the back gently.

"Don't worry, we will fix all of this." She sighed and added. "I feel like I've said, 'I'll fix' This too much today. It's time to actually deliver.", She said.

Tallah reached up and lovingly touched Vera's arm. Lastly Vera caressed Koi's shoulders on her way back to the stove.

"But first, we eat." She said as she took four bowls from the cabinet.

The next days' work flew by quickly, but their minds were all tense. None more so than Vera, she had her council meeting beginning almost instantly when school let out. She'd have enough time to do her weekly deep clean of the room and walk there.

Koi came into the room while Vera was stooped over sweeping out from under a desk. The beautiful handmade broom she used was woven with red thread and had been an item she'd traded a painting for last year at the Hooni day festival. It was not only functional, but Vera hung it on the wall between uses. It was an art piece. Soft broom sage with sprigs of purple, yellow, and red steams of various plants intermingled into an arc that led to a pointed end that Vera thought was useful for those hard-to-reach places behind corners and under shelves. The tiny decorative seashells that were sewn onto the area below where her hand was to grip could be heard tinkling with each movement.

Koi stood and watched her. Her motions were like poetry in motion. The *swish swish* of the broom along with the tinkling of the shells added to this moment. Creating a performance piece out of the simple act.

When she looked up to see Koi silently standing and watching her, she didn't smile, or issue any normal politeness, she just stood very still. He didn't speak either, neither needed to. They both understood the weight of today's meeting and knew that what Vera faced would be difficult and it would once again have to be without him or Tallah. You can't plan for the unknown, so today would be another wild ride. He hugged her and tried to give her all the strength he could in that one hug.

Entering the council building Vera passed the hallway holding the offices belonging to the head council members who exclusively worked on Dayak matters, the rest had other regular jobs and didn't need an office. The end of the hallway opened to its massive meeting hall. This room could hold over 500 hooni. It's high vaulted ceilings and stone floor gave it a grand appearance. Today it seemed to lack its grandiose appeal and was replaced with a feeling of Forebodingness.

Despite the difference in the way she felt towards today's meeting it ran no differently. Food was laid out on tables at the back, Everyhooni ate and exchanged pleasantries. Vera found the idol small talk difficult to focus on with all the other drama intensely pounding in her head.

Lady Vazeet sat down beside Vera, she'd positioned herself halfway up the rows of chairs and on the aisle seat. Vera acknowledged her with a nod of her head.

Thankfully her mouth was full, so she didn't feel required to say anything. The old woman also silently ate.

Vera soon understood why lady Vazeet had sat beside her when she caught sight of Lorn pacing at the far side of the room, his gaze burning a hole through them. As the members of the senior council of wisdom began to take their chairs at the high table Vazeet covertly put her hand on Vera's knee. It would have looked to anyhooni who'd happened to see as an aided attempt to stand by an old woman. The quick squeeze let Vera know otherwise.

"Breathe, be steady girl." Lady Vazeet whispered before letting go and taking her place at the high table.

The trivial matters were handled first as always. Vera almost missed when head of council, ZaLee asked her if the 'school had its Hooni day project underway.' She had luckily put a group of teachers in charge of it this year, so it wasn't hers to worry over.

"Yes, it's coming along." Was her response in an upbeat way.

Lorn could hardly sit still, Vera was paying very close attention to him. If councilman Een shifted one inch that may indicate he was going to bring his issue to the floor Lorn would move to the edge of his seat. It was obvious he wanted to get the jump on that topic. Vera also noticed every time he'd do that Lady Vazeet would grin to herself. It felt nice knowing she had an alliance with her.

Head of animal affairs gave a lengthy speech about how sightings of creatures great and small that normally avoided our populated areas were concerning and that we should all document them and tell everyone in our pods to do the same.

"Bring these paper records of animal sightings to me at the next meeting. I'm looking for patterns and clues as to why." He finally sat down leaving the floor open.

To which Lorn wasted no time claiming. He began with his usual politeness that Vera could now see was hallow and a sham.

"Good day, nice to see all you wonderful Hooni again today. I look forward to these meetings more than any other part of my week. It's such an honor to be among you. As a concerned member of this island, I've lost a lot of sleep over the thought that we have Hooni that are not responding to the therapeutic treatments that have worked for Everyhooni since the dawn of our society.

"Councilman Een's proposal to remove them from our land and cast them out like Pariahs isn't sitting well with me. I can't allow such horrible acts to happen. So after much deliberation I've devised an alternative. I propose that these Hooni are simply sick, I ask that you give them to me." He cleared just throat and rephrased his last statement.

"Give them to the L.A.B.S. allow me, uh, our team of gifted scientists to try and figure out how we can help restore these poor hooni to full functionality."

He smiled and extended his arm towards the crowd, "shall we vote by show of hands."
As the crowd began to mumble and shift in their chairs, head of council ZaLee, started to raise his hand in favor when Lady Vazeet leapt to her feet in strong objection.

"Absolutely not Lorn!" She walked around in front of the table to where he stood and addressed the room.

"Am I the onlyhooni that sees flaw in this, not only have we not heard both sides and any other options but since when did Lorn take the leaders post in this group? To many liberties are being taken these days by him and others."

Lorn opened his mouth to begin a rebuttal but in her unapologetic manner she shut him up quickly.

"Don't even try boy. I'd also like to ask how many Hooni knew about this proposal of Lorns' before today? Because personally I did. I also know a few others of you did too. We cannot let our world crumble beneath our feet. I'm very disappointed." She turned and fixed her eyes on him. His ability to smile at her and play nice turned Vera's stomach.

"Now Lady Vazeet, I'm sorry if you thought I acted in any way unscrupulously, I was seeking your wisdom since I was so deeply concerned..."

he was talking to the crowd like an actor delivering a monologue on stage. It was at this moment that Vera could no longer hold her seat nor her tongue. Jumping from her chair with enough force make the legs screech across the floor.

"What's your excuse then for asking me Lorn?" Vera nearly yelled so that the whole room could hear.

He quickly snatched back the ear of the room. "Well you tend to think outside of the box and I was hoping by talking to you about it that I'd gain insight as to..."

Once again, he was cut off. It was becoming comical with the back and forth of Vazeet and Vera playing catch with his speeches.

"Outside of the box?" Lady Vazeet spat. "What are you playing at Lorn? Is that a sideways attempt at calling her UnHooni? Perhaps you'd like her to be turned over to the L.A.B.S. as well? Or me, tread lightly hence forth." Her hunter gatherer accent was strong in the last sentence.

Lorn attempted once again to regain control over the situation. "Now I didn't mean to ruffle you ladies. No, I don't run anything. We all know that councilman ZaLee is our head and I'm just doing my civil duty to our community. Forgive me for not following proper order. Please, let's handle this in the correct way. Tell me why we shouldn't help these Hooni."

To apologize and back down like this was misdirection at its finest. It now put the pressure on the rest of the room to come up with reasons why the L.A.B.S. *shouldn't* get the wayward Hooni. Why they should be exiled and not helped.

Lady Vazeet stole a look at Vera expressing her shock. The two realized they'd been played by Lorn, and like good puppets they'd preformed just as he scripted.

Councilman Een quickly took the floor. His hasty grab at the attention of the room made Vera know that somehow, he was an Ally to them on some unseen level.

"These Hooni in question are NOT sick. They are about as UnHooni as possible. Without being disrespectful to Lorn, but he IS the focus of their anger for some reason. It would be to his detriment to release these hooni to his care. I fear they could Legitimately hurt him or others."

It was then that Vera knew just what to propose. She waited though to let a few more voices be heard before she spoke. She knew her time was coming, and she needed to take the correct window.

"Evicting them is really the only solution I feel comfortable with." One explained.

"Can't they just stay where they are, and we keep trying what's always worked. Maybe they just need more time." Added another.

Lorn sat quietly and faked a concerned look on his face bobbing his head from one speaker to the next like he had a front row seat at a tennis match.When Lotta spoke, she wove a tapestry of the virtue of the L.A.B.S., how their lives are healthy and safe thanks to the work they do.

"...and least you all not forget what fate befell the humans. If these hooni are sick and we don't act they may be the seed that becomes the downfall of us all. We must think of the children of Dayak." She sat down with an air of judgment as she cast her gaze over the room.

"I think we should let Lorn and the L.A.B.S. take them. It's our hooni duty to restore them and return them to life." Declared the head of council. It appeared that he was about to put it to a final vote among the room.

Lady Vazeet looked desperately at Vera. Great moments often spring from planning and having all the needed ducks in a row. This one however just sprang.

"Absolutely not!" All heads turned to Vera, who was once again standing, and this time was yelling so all could hear. "I propose we bring the Hooni in question here and hear from them before making a decision that affects someone else's life so profoundly."

Lorn stood and spoke. His voice was no longer as calm and pleasant as he'd maintained earlier. "Because they're dangerous and I won't put this room in jeopardy to prove it Vera!"

Vera continued to be bold and push the line. "Or is it that you don't want a room full of us to hear why they supposedly hate you?"

Lotta didn't rise but yelled, "you've got some nerve girl."

Lorn smiled in an eerie manner as he tried to remain in control of the situation. Obviously being talked to like this in a public setting wasn't something he was prepared for either.

"Poor little Vera. I *HAVE* been worried about you lately, this ladies and gentleman is what I suspect are the first symptoms of our mystery illness." He motioned at two members of the L.A.B.S. representatives that sat at the back of the room. As they slowly walked towards her so did councilman Een, and Lady Vazeet.

Vera wasted no time in her reply. "Wait a minute." She screamed. "It isn't me that you need to worry about. It's this room full of Hooni who are about to find out what you really are that you should worry about. Explain to this room why you've not returned my student for days after his third strike. Tell them how you are controlling us all and using the hunter gatherer Pods like your own work force." She turned and saw the two hooni getting closer, so she ramped up her volume and speed.

"Please believe me. I'm not sick, Lorn is diabolical. We are indeed all in danger but it's because of him!"

Lorns' calm demeanor was starting to fall away. "This girl doesn't know what she's talking about. She's probably contagious too. Let's get her out of here for the good of hoonikind."

By Vera's next statements Vazeet and Een had reached her side. "No, I am NOT sick. The fact that he wants me gone so readily should be a concern to all of you." She turned to look at the faces of the room. Some looked scared or concerned. Others looked angry. At the back of the hallway near the offices she saw Tallah, Koi, and Nash. They'd been there listening the whole time. They too now ran to Vera as she spoke.

"Please, listen. He keeps the hunter, fisher, and gathering pods in near destitution. Their homes aren't upgraded, he takes their children for corrective therapy at unprecedentedly higher rates more so than other Hooni. He physically hurt me and Tallah at the garden and I've heard him yelling and threatening the head hunter. It didn't start with him though. His whole family has blood on their hands." The room was stone silent. Een began to talk.

"What Vera says is true! The L.A.B.S. are NOT our guardians or protection as we once thought." Een yelled.

Vera was grateful and more than a little surprised. Een continued.

"He's out for power! I saw him trying to get into the water supply's filtration room months ago. He had containers of chemicals intended to be spread to each of us! Luckily our head of water does an amazing job at locking the tanks up."

Een looked towards Taga, the woman who oversaw water for all of Dayak. She stood up without hesitation. Obviously angry,

"It's true, we noticed all access points to our water plant being tampered with over a year ago. We assumed that it was animals seeking the water, so we upped our safety measures. Once councilman Een told me that Lorn was in fact the animal so desperately trying to get at the water supply we upgraded everything to make sure it was tamper proof."

Lorn leered at the room and pointed his finger directly at Vera and the five others that now surrounded her.

"This is ridiculous. She is contagious, they all are, we all need to get out of here. Return to your pods at once. Do not leave until an official L.A.B.S. member comes and gives you the all clear." Then he added, "Manitu and Cleep, please grab them." He instructed his two L.A.B.S. members who'd now made it to where Vera stood. About a Hundred Hooni stood and walked obediently to the exit. Many however did not.

Someone yelled, "Lorn if this isn't true tell me why the pods aren't upgraded like she said! I've seen them too!"

More Hooni began shouting about little things they'd noticed. It was apparent that Vera, Koi, and Tallah were not the only ones who'd been woke up. Yet still the hundred or so who'd wanted to walk out were being held from leaving at the doorway by the larger group of agitated Hooni. The retreating Hooni kept asking politely

"Please let me pass." Or "I need to return to my pod for Hooni safety." They didn't yell or push. Just strangely insisted.
Vera once again opened her mouth and yelled. "Can anyone say that their behavior is normal?"

She challenged the room while pointing to the group trying to leave. The angry Hooni turned their attention to the zombie like hooni at the back. Taga lifted her cup to her nose and sniffed it.

"We've been drugged, who was in charge of the punch?" Taga yelled. Lady Natuk who normally headed the food preparation pointed at the elder council table.

"Lotta volunteered for it today. She told me I deserved a break and that she felt like she'd not done enough of her hooni duty lately."

Lorn saw his whole master plan unraveling before him. "I said return to your pods!" He yelled. Shockingly more hooni who'd not obeyed the first time went rigid and walked towards the exit. Their push for the door was gentle but their numbers made it impossible for the other non-compliant Hooni to hold them back.

Lorn yelled again, "Wait, this sickness is hard to control." He told the obedient hooni who stopped and waited eagerly for his direction. "For your safety and the safety of others you who are not sick must mark yourself. So that we may know at a distance who's affected and who's safe. I command that you remove your shoes now as an outward sign and when you get to your home shave your heads. It will be another marker of the unsick."
About two hundred hooni removed their shoes and continued towards the exit.

"Power corrupts and absolute power corrupts absolutely." Lady Vazeet yelled. The remaining few unaltered hooni shifted to allow the others to leave. It was like a flock of birds turning and diving in unison. The ones filling out now pulled and jerked away from the ones staying. They were afraid of them; it was as if they really saw the rest as sick and dangerous.

"Shut the building from the outside when you leave" he yelled to the small army he'd ordered to go home. "This problem needs to be taken care of now."

The hallways had now been cleared and the buildings large doors at the front could now be heard being closed.

"Alpha team, come and help me." Lorn yelled, his voice echoing down the hallway. From inside the offices of Lotta and ZaLee came dozens of Hooni with club like sticks. They'd obviously been drugged first and had stood in wait for the command to act.

The Alpha team, as Lorn has called them, marched into the room, and lined up at the only exit. Tallah began to quickly move among the group of hooni that now huddled on the opposite side of the room from the Alpha team. From her pouch that was around her waist she pulled out white balls about the size of large grapes. She put one in everyhooni's hand. Telling them to follow her lead when the time comes.

Lady Vazeet likewise was passing a message around the group as fast as she could also. "Meet back at the rivers fork in the hunter gather area."

For everyone in that group, fear now clutched at their hearts. They'd never expected to be in this situation. Nothing in their lives had ever prepared them for a moment that would require them to fight back.

# CHAPTER TEN

Lorn and Lotta had been talking loudly but no one had paid them much attention until Lorn yelled at head of council, ZaLee. What he'd said hadn't been understood but ZaLee instantly walked to the nearest chair and sat down.

"Well mother it's been a long road, but our time has finally came. What should we do with the genetically resistance group?" He asked

She chuckled slightly and answered, "Kill them. No wounds, do it with the gas so that we can have the other Hooni see their bodies. It will help sell this 'mystery illness to anyone else that can't be genetically controlled."

"Yes Mother." He smiled and looked at the group. "I will do what you said, with the exception of that one." Pointing at Vera while he looked back over his shoulder at his Lotta.

She sighed and said, "Fine, do as you wish. No one will miss her anyway. We killed her mother and father years ago."

Koi grabbed Vera's hand as Lotta and Lorn continued to talk.
"The father was much easier to kill. He and his band of men were snooping around me and my father's work. Dad started a fire at the farm and they ran straight into their death trying be a hero. It was a great way to get rid of a bunch of damming evidence against us too. Oh, and that Ones parents too," she said as she pointed at Koi who now held Vera against his chest.

"Their fathers were easy to get rid of, but their mothers were L.A.B.S. scientists and they almost were our downfall. Until I perfected that gas that gave me such a clean kill with no residue." She fluffed her hair with her hand while talking. It was such a casual tone to the whole confession that just made Vera sick.

"I knew she started that fire, the evil beast." Vazeet said seething.

She then placed her hands on Vera and Koi's back. "When we get out of here meet back where the rivers fork behind the hunters stands. Time to fight is here kids."

Nash and Tallah stood by lady Vazeet with Vera and Koi in front of them. Tallah didn't feel like standing in line to be slaughtered by some mysterious gas. Action needed to be taken.

"Get ready guys." She said softly.

Lotta and Lorn turned to walk towards the entrance, the alpha team parted to let them pass and Vera began to yell at them.

"You cowards. Come back!" They turned and took bait.

"You insignificant pissant." Lotta spat. "Lorn, get your toy before I gas her along with the rest of them."

Lorn smiled and he and his mother walked directly up to the resistant group. Lotta pulled a single syringe from her pocket as Lorn grabbed Vera by the arm, her reaction was instantaneous. She bit him! Jerking her arm up and her head down in one motion she sunk her teeth into his hand. She then bulldogged her head ripping some of the flesh from him.

It was at that moment that Tallah screamed, "NOW!" She threw her little ball and a giant cloud of white smoke erupted. It was followed by more from all the hooni in the group.

The smoke was disorienting. They shoved Lorn and Lotta over and used the Chaotic room to their advantage, pushing past the Alpha team that blocked the door. The grand meeting hall with its high ceilings and stone floor was an echo chamber of disaster for Lorn and Lotta who now screamed orders at their army. The army couldn't see, nor could they hear over the voices and shuffling of frantic hooni trying to escape. Like polite hooni they stood still and stoic as they'd previously been told to, while the resistant members of the room all got away virtually unharmed.

Vera ran like she'd never ran before. She stopped at the entrances to pods she'd pass and yell that 'Lorn and Lotta were evil.' That 'every hooni are in danger' after stopping at a few pods it had given her friends a chance to catch up to her. They begged her to come on and hurry up.

"We have to get to safety." Koi said in a demanding tone.

"Go I'm coming, I can outrun all of you. Don't stop." She yelled back.


Several pods later Lady Vazeet and Een came walking as fast as they could past her on their way to the meeting place.

"Come on child, NOW!" Vazeet screamed at Vera.

"I have to warn the other Hooni, I'm coming." She said while running towards the next pod.

"NOW VERA!" Vazeet bellowed.

The shock made her listen. Een quickly told her. "Vera, they can't be helped, most won't believe you. You're wasting time. Plus, I have a way to tell the whole island at once. I just have to get to the corrections facility." Vazeet must have sensed the hesitation Vera had to trust Een.

"He's on our side." She said passionately

"But he wanted to exile the hooni at the corrections facility." Vera said almost in tears. Finally allowing the situation to wash over her.

"Vera, I lied, I was going to release them into the jungle. To start our resistance. They knew everything. They are the ones that opened my eyes to Lorn and Lotta. Lady Vazeet and I have been working towards this moment. We will not give up this island to Lorn and Lotta and their twisted family. I promise. Trust me, let's go!" Een pleaded with her.

Vazeet added, "run ahead. Start talking to the resistant hooni who are gathering, tell them what you know. Tell Nash to gather the hunters and everyone he can. Spread the news through our pods. We can win this but be aware that you just signed up for war kidlet!"

Vera looked at their faces and reluctantly understood that yelling at each pod was indeed futile. So, she simply said, "okay." And took off for the gathering place.

The trees and pods entrances near the path flashed by in a blur. Her mind was going even faster than her feet. The gathering stall came into view, and she saw that no one was working at them. Vera assumed that some other hooni had grabbed them to come to the river fork. Vera continued around behind the stall, still running. Within seconds she could see the wide sandy banks that held in the beautiful river. The hooni that were gathered there were mostly the ones from the meeting that were resistant. A few others from the gathering pods had joined them, attracted obviously by the commotion. A few of the older hooni from the meeting, like Een and Vazeet hadn't made it yet. Vera hoped they'd be here soon.

Being a leader is oftentimes a roll someone grows into, but for this instance 'leader' was something Vera had to embody immediately. Still in full run she leapt onto a large boulder and loudly started telling the hooni around her what was what.

"I'm Vera, I know everyone is scared but here's the information I have. The L.A.B.S. are our enemy! Do not hesitate to run from them. Or fight back if you can! They WILL kill you if they get the chance! Lotta and Lorn have lost what little of their blasted minds they had! They've assembled an army; they're calling them the Alpha team. All hooni affected will most likely have no shoes, or hair! However, if he hands out more of his new medication, it could change anyone who's susceptible to it, they become unable to disobey him.

"Although, from what we experienced in the council meeting, if they can't hear him, he can't control them. So be loud! They have a gas, it's deadly and undetectable. Avoid being inside anywhere. Open air seems safer."

She paused and looked around at the faces gazing up at her. Some were scared, most were nodding in agreement. Silently joining their own army for hooni freedom. Vera saw Nash's sister and Deevids mom,

"Kajaah and Rhoan will you please gather ALL mothers and their small kids and head somewhere safe in the jungle with them!" She asked.

Rhoan yelled back, "Absolutely, we'll protect the kids at all costs! We'll head for the base hunting camp at the foot of the mountain. There are caves to our back there and a wide river in front of it. It will be the safest place."

Vera felt a rush of relief, somehow this may work.

"Okay everyhooni here now knows where the kids will be, should you become injured, or unable to fight you too go to the base camp with Rhoan and Kajaah. This will be EVERYHOONI's fallback place!"

She looked to her right and saw Tallah and Nash standing behind Koi. She wanted to send them to the safety of the base camp along with the children, but sadly knew she couldn't do that. She saw a few of the women going with Kajaah and Rhoan. They weren't wasting any time.

Vera turned to Nash and Bip. "You guys are two of the best hunters. I'm putting you in charge of the actual fighting. I'd like to suggest you set up over there and teach us any skill you think could be beneficial. I know it's a lot to process, but anything in regard to the jungle, or absolutely any knowledge you have that may keep one of us alive. Oh, and what about weapons. We'll need things to defend ourselves." The word 'weapon' seemed foreign in her mouth. Making her almost sick as it crossed her lips.

Nash responded Seamlessly though, "The spears we hunt with, and knifes for the fish stalls will make excellent personal defense weapons!" He says as he runs off to gather them up.

She grabs Tallah by the hand and pulls her up onto the rock. "Tallah made, um... she gave us, I'm not sure what it was..." she stumbled for the first time over her thoughts and looked at Tallah. Luckily Tallah picked up where Vera fell short.

"I have a large bag with tiny poof balls in it. Every hooni should get some from me. I can easily make more. It's based on puff ball mushrooms. When you throw them or pop them a large cloud of white dust comes out. I spent all day making them." She turned and spoke directly to Vera, "I felt like something massive was about to happen."

Vera grabbed her hand and squeezed it lovingly. Tallah was so smart, she was happy her friends strange love of mushrooms and her quick thinking created these poof balls.

"Good thing too" she answered Then went back to addressing the crowd.

"Een says he has a way of getting a message to the whole island, but he'll have to have help to get to the corrections facility to do it. I need someone to volunteer to help get him there once he arrives. He and Lady Vazeet were just behind me. Okay... okay..." she paused and searched her mind for anything she may have forgotten.

"Lorn, is calling his army Alpha. It's an ancient word for 'the start or beginning.' He won't win, we won't let him. This isn't the start of anything except our awakening. The original omega team feared their world was ending. Now Lorn thinks he's beginning a new world. Let's show him what we think of his new world order shall we! I'd like to tell you all, we'll be okay. But truth is, we won't all be standing when it's over. If you don't want to fight, go to the mountain with the kids now! I won't force anyone into anything. There's no shame in not fighting, but please be helpful somehow at base camp.

"Also, in honor of two women who lost their lives a long time ago trying to stop the L.A.B.S., I declare this group of the resistant hooni be forever called the 'KaiNaandi' may we all travel safely and see each other when the smoke clears."

She pushed down the lump in her throat, wiped the tears from her eyes and jumped down to hug Koi and Tallah before heading over to get her spear from Nash.

Suddenly two children came running into the midst of everyhooni lining up for weapons. They were shaking like leaves and terrified. Vera recognized them as Tayah and Reelah, Rhoan's oldest daughters. Vera grabbed the scared children and asked what had happened.

"L.A.B.S." they managed to say between gasping for breath.

Vera told them to wait, "I need you to tell everyone, come here." She lifted Reelah onto the rock. "Go on, please tell them loudly."

The girl was very upset by whatever had happened but nevertheless she was loud and clear. Her bravery made Vera hopeful that they had a chance.

"People from the L.A.B.S. came to the park where we had stopped to play. They made everyone line up to take a medication. They said that a dangerous sickness had begun and that if we'd take this pill now we'd not catch it. Almost everyhooni took it. We hid, so did a few others we saw."

she paused and gestured to herself and sister. "Once everyhooni had taken it, the L.A.B.S. member told them in an angry voice to 'return to their pods. That they needed to remove their shoes, to prevent spreading the bacteria that's found on the ground, and to shave their head to show they'd taken the medication. Then everyone just did it. They didn't talk or ask anything, just slid their shoes off and turned and left the park."

Koi asked, loud enough to be heard by all. "How many Hooni were there, and did they see you?"

"No one saw us," the girl answered. "We were sitting in a large tree when the L.A.B.S. members in their white coats walked into the park. We said nothing when we saw them. We also waited till they'd left before we ran home. Maybe fifty hooni were at the park."

Vera thanked them for their information. Also told them where they'd find their mother. Then climbed back into the rock herself to address the crowd again having had a new idea that needed to be heard.

"Okay, Lorn and his alpha team are probably going everywhere giving Hooni these pills. It's safe to say that most will become Alpha. KaiNaadi has an advantage though. A lot of the food Dayak eats comes from here. I ask that several of you go make up a bunch of parcels. Just something everyone can put into a nap sack to be carried with them to eat. Then all the other food supplies should be wrapped up and sent with the groups of women heading to the mountain base camp. The top foraging people need to go to that camp as well. You will be of better service to KaiNaadi by keeping us fed than in battle. Tallah, I want you to go organize and be in charge of that please. You can also set up a lab of your own to make poof balls and other things at the base camp."

Vera knew that Tallah was systematic and logical in her thinking and would be a great asset to them there. Also, Vera was glad she could try and keep at least one person she loved safe.

"I need a group to volunteer to go to ALL the pods here in the Hunter, fisher and gathering area and tell them to come here or head to the mountain base camp. Also tell them to take anything with them that may be helpful, we don't know if we'll be back to our homes soon. Have them send us backpacks or waist pouches... anything our soldiers, can carry with them in the jungle."

Calling these hooni soldiers made her stomach sick. Pictures of humans crouched in camouflage killing one another flashed across her mind.

"I am not sure, but I think Lorn is making the hooni remove their shoes so that if the medication doesn't make them Alpha, at least they can't run to the jungle. Have everyone gather extra shoes and send them here too along with the bags if possible." She said as she climbed down yet again.

With each decision she made the anger that had been stifled and tamed inside her grew and found its way to the surface. Her knowledge of history, humans, and her one-of-a-kind mind now found its purpose as she took the leadership position of the KaiNaandi.

Lady Vazeet and Een along with a few other older hooni who'd been slower now arrived. Vera quickly filled them in on what had been started. Koi and an older but fit looking hunter came to stand beside Vera.

"We're going to be Een's escort to the corrections facility. How is it that you can get a message to all of Dayak from there?" The older hunter asked.

Happy that his traveling company had been assembled already he explained. "When the Omega team had settled here, they had an air raid siren with them. It's basically a very loud speaker. The group of people at the facility have been working on it. So that we can speak through it and not just sound a single alarm sound. Most people will be able to hear it.

I've also had these hooni making weapons for a few months. If we can reach them before Lorn, we stand a greater chance of success against The Alpha team. Hopefully the hooni there will be able defend themselves should the Alpha team reach them first; however I don't think the corrections facility will be on Lorn's radar. He thinks they're locked up, he has no idea the extent of what I've been doing with them."

Vera didn't really have time to grasp the whole picture that Een was on the side of the KaiNaadi or that he'd been working to form a militaristic group of hooni from the hardest to control of the population. It was genuinely ingenious.

She turned to Lady Vazeet. "I need you to go to the base camp. Help me run that operation. Tallah is already heading the defense lab and rationing portion from there but there's so much more needed than I've even thought of."

Lady Vazeet told her she'd go, but that she needed to speak with her before she left. "But first I'll give you a minute with Koi, before he leaves." She walked away leaving Koi and Vera in Simi-privacy.

The two just fell into each other. Both knew the others heart. No amount of words could match the feelings of their hug. Koi broke the hug first. He pulled Vera back and wiped the tears from her face with his palm. She turned her head so that her lips kissed his hand as he turned to walk away.

"I'll see you when this is over" he said. "...and I'm marring you, no more delays!"

Vera yelled after him, "I love you Koi! I'll be waiting!"

After Koi, Een, and the old hunter named Grupth had disappeared from sight, lady Vazeet returned to Vera side.

She loudly announced. "No matter what group you're from, we are all family now! Once you have your weapons come receive a mark. This is a gathers tradition and it's an honor to receive. It's my hope that you wear it as a badge of your courage and may it remind you that your part of something bigger than yourself.

"My brothers and sisters, the Alpha are set on our Genocide, but 'we will not go easily into that goodnight' I as elder among us, officially declare Vera not only our leader, but the face for a future without mindless obedience. She has never EVER had one drop of medication from the L.A.B.S. and will be a key to our outthinking them. Travel safely brethren."

She ended her spirit boosting speech and turned without pause to mark Vera's cheeks and between her eyebrows with a beautiful dark brown symbol. These were marks she'd always admired and would now wear with pride.

"How'd you know I was never administered anything by the L.A.B.S.?" Vera asked with some level of suspicion.

She answered hurriedly but warmly. "Kai had come and told me everything shortly before she was murdered. I've been keeping an eye on you kidlet. She'd be proud, now go!"

# CHAPTER ELEVEN

Vera did just that. She went and directed armed hooni into trees and other places for ambushed attacks on the Alpha with Nash and Bip helping and more hunters and gathers turning up from the pods with weapons and knowledge of the woods. They were soon dispersed in small groups everywhere around the entrance to the woods. They'd force the Alpha to come to them. The fishing and trapping nets were set up along the path that extended from where they were in the jungles' edge towards the stalls. Some on the ground with spring triggers and others from the trees suspended above the path to fall from above.

It had been around two hours when suddenly a loud wailing sound echoed through the air. Followed by Eens' voice.

"All hooni, now hear this, now hear this! L.A.B.S. has been corrupted from the inside. They're going to turn us ALL into slaves! There is NO sickness, do NOT take their medication. Do not drink public water sources! Come to the hunter gatherer pods and join the resistance before it's too late! They WILL kill you. You must fight and run!" Then the wailing siren began again. When it's last echo fell silent it was as if the whole world didn't exist. You could have heard a feather fall to the jungle floor.

Vera was happy to know that Koi and his little team had made it. Hopefully they could also make it back. There was again, very little time to devote to any other thought because the silence was shattered by a thundering of feet that could be heard down the path before the stalls.

She wanted to yell something to all the hooni around her to make sure they knew the enemy was approaching, but she knew silence was more important. Her heartbeat thumped in her ears, and she could feel the vessels to the side of her neck racing. This was it.

A group of hooni, maybe a hundred strong rounded the curve and proceeded to the first pod which was visible from Vera's vantage point in the tree she was perched in. They marched in an out of sync manner, together but uncoordinatedly. They ripped open doors and could be heard ransacking the houses obviously in search of the KaiNaandi.

They had found no hooni since all had fled earlier. The group of Alpha returned to the path closer to where all the KaiNaandi sat nervously ready. They began to walk towards the next set of pods when they stepped into a net. At least 20 Alpha zoomed upwards carried aloft by the strong thick net. The rest looked but did not act. They resumed their march towards the next pods on the path. Vera was shocked. The Alpha made no attempt to help their fellow hooni in the nets, just walked on to continue their mission. The hooni in the net wiggled but made no sounds or real attempt to free themselves either. The power of obedience Lorn had turned on must have removed their ability to have any other senses.

It had been a tense twenty minutes or so and most of the netted Alpha had now found comfortable spots. Sitting with their legs out of the nets, back-to-back and in other positions verses the dogpile that had occurred when they'd first been wadded up with the nets initial snatch into the air. The other Alpha were out of earshot. Everyone knew they'd probably continued checking all the pods deeper into the woods.

It was in this false calmness that Vera saw the unimaginable. A young hooni climbed down from her spot in a tree nearer to the net. She tentatively walked onto the path and touched the bare feet of a young alpha female that sat suspended in the net. With a hopeful sound she called the captive Alpha by name.

"Mangtie, oh my goodness. It IS you. I was so worried." The girl obviously recognized this Alpha as a close friend. She talked at her with no response in return. Vera was torn. Her mind turning towards what she'd have done if Tallah had been in the net, but this didn't feel safe.

A larger hunter began to climb down next to Vera, he looked at her on his way down and whispered, "it's my kid sister and our little cousin. They're inseparable." Vera didn't know what to do but climbed down also.

They'd almost stepped out of the jungle onto the path when the Alpha in the net began to speak. Vera and the hunter froze to hear her words.

"Take you're medication." Was the only thing she said and extended her hand outward through the net with a pill in it. The KaiNaandi girl refused and was attempting to reason with Mangtie when she started yelling.

"Infected Hooni!" the Alpha continued to yell the same words over and over again. Vera and the hunter ran towards the young KaiNaandi who stood frozen in shock looking up at her cousin who now didn't even seem to recognize her when a group of Alpha came from the stalls area. Vera had had no clue that more Alpha soldiers had been waiting silently at the other end of the path. No one could have.

In a swirl of chaos Vera saw hooni jumping down from trees as the Alpha soldier struck the young KaiNaandi across the head with a clubbed stick. The girl fell heavily to the ground. Blood pooling around her cracked skull. She was instantly dead. The mission of the Alpha was clear and undeniable. If anyhooni had doubted that these Alpha would kill, that had been wiped away in that terrible moment.

The KaiNaadi didn't hesitate. They fought hard. Dropping Alpha soldiers left and right. The ones in the net yelled, "infected hooni!" Loudly and continued yelling it endlessly. The first group who'd went to search pods were now back called in by the cry of "infected hooni" they too joined in the battle.

Vera saw a hunter with two Alpha swinging their clubs at him. He held them off with his spear but an obviously broken arm, undoubtedly from a blow by another Alpha's club made it difficult for him. Vera took a palm sized rock and beamed one of them in the side of the head and speared the other one. She stood beside the wounded hunter.

"Thank you, Vera." He said. The two stood panting. Vera addressed the hunter without looking at him, keeping her eyes on the danger that may come from anywhere.

"I need you to fall back to the base camp. Tell them what's happening. Get your arm seen to. Warn them that the war is in the jungle now. No Alpha can be trusted, even if you know them. Drop a poof ball once you get a few hundred feet away, so no Alpha try to follow your retreat."

He did as he was asked and just like that he was gone. Vera had all but worn herself out. She sat down at the base of a tree. No sooner had she let her body go slack than a bald Alpha emerged from the right side of a thicket in front of her. The woman was panting, obviously tired too. She didn't let that stop her though. She flung herself at Vera. She had no clubbed weapon as the others had had, maybe it had been lost in another battle. The Alpha was on top of Her trying to force her hand close to Vera's face.

Vera lost her grip on the Alpha's shoulder and found the woman's hands around her mouth. She was trying to put her fingers into Vera's mouth. It dawned on Vera, no, not her fingers she was trying to put the pills into her mouth.

The strength that the woman had was hard to match. They were both tired, but the free Will was absent from the Alpha. They may very well follow orders till the body died of exhaustion. With her last ounce of strength Vera brought her thick leg up and around the assailant perched on her stomach. In one swift move she knocked the woman off and used the leverage to change positions. Making herself now sitting on the Alpha holding her down.

"I don't want to hurt you." Vera cried.

The woman went limp and didn't struggle. She looked into Vera's eyes and for a split second and Vera thought there was a flicker of conciseness. If there was it had been fleeting. She thrust her head forward cracking it into Vera's cheekbone. She began to yell "infected hooni."

Before Vera had time to think she pulled the curved blade from her waistband and dragged it across the Alpha's neck. Vera hit hard and fast. Blood speckled across her face.

The Alpha went still, and Vera had to fight the Urge to scream and freak out over this very violent and close kill. She could hear several Alpha moving closing to her, beckoned in by the screams of 'infected hooni.'

Vera turned to run and threw a poof ball behind her to hide her direction.

"Thank you Tallah." She said to herself.

Hoping inside that no harm would come to those she loved yet knowing she herself just caused harm to someone's loved one made her heart ache. The battle had been going on for over an hour. Vera had gone to a large clearing surrounded by a thick wall of banana trees. This had been their agreed meeting place. Bip had shown or told everyone where this was when they'd been giving out weapons and advice.

The circle inside the banana trees was a perfect hiding spot. The mother trees and their pups formed a tight circle with only one real entrance. Which Bip had said they kept cut out. Kids played in these as a pretend house and hunters napped in them occasionally. It was massive but felt very cozy. Slowly more and more KaiNaandi trickled in. Some limped or were supported by others but most came in under their own power. Other than scrapes the majority seemed unharmed. It was a relief to Vera.

They all exchanged stories and compared notes. Plans were made to take the injured to the base camp under the cover of darkness, which was quickly coming.

"Vera" a familiar voice said behind her.

She jumped from the ground and flung herself around Koi so quickly she knocked the wind out of herself a little bit. She didn't care though. He was here and safe!

Just then Een and loads of others from the corrections facility had entered the banana haven. They carried metal boxes and other objects that could only have been the device that Een had made the announcement over. Handmade weapons filled bags carried by the others. Some of the hooni rejoiced at seeing the ones from the correctional facility, obviously they'd been family separated for some time now.

Vera briefed Een and Koi. Then Koi let Een tell Vera about their trip to and from the facility, which had really been uneventful. He told her that he and the older men carrying the loudspeaker were about to head to the base camp.

"We're just dropping off soldiers for the KaiNaandi and more weapons that we have made at the facility over the last few months." Then he simply said goodbye and he and his new little group, along with the injured left the safety of the banana circle and walked out of sight towards the mountain.

Vera stood in a small impassable gap between the banana trees, a large leaf hung directly over her head. It's broad green umbrella like presence made her feel smaller than normal. She looked up as the last waves of sunlight shone down on them. Looking at the underside of the leaf the light illuminated the veins and ribs that fed it and gave it strength. It was a simple moment of undeniable beauty amidst the ugliness of her current reality.

Koi told her that he'd seen a large pile of dead hooni outside of the L.A.B.S. facility as they'd made their way back here. There were several piles of hundreds all near the crematorium building. (Hooni were never buried, no land was to be wasted. Omega had built a beautiful building to honor the dead who were respectfully cremated.)

"Bald Alpha were carting the dead inside unceremoniously. Some of the dead were bald, others were not. Lorn is killing everyone. It was sickening. The dead weren't bloody. I'm assuming they died by gas, or something." Koi told her.

The whole group of KaiNaandi had fallen silent to listen to Koi. One of the men from the corrections facility spoke up.

"That medication can kill too. It's powers to alter the brain into submission is more than some of us can handle. I watched it kill my roommate at the facility before Een started limiting what Lorn could do inside there." He explained.

Vera took some fruit from her bag and handed it to him.

"Everyone feed our brethren from the corrections facility. Not that you need to be reminded to share, it is our nature after all. We'll sleep now, sleeping in turns to keep watch. I volunteer for first watch. If you have any questions, suggestions, or anything at all to aid your KaiNaandi brethren please come to me immediately! Everyone is unique, and what you could add to our plight may be our success."

"I have something." A voice from outside of the banana trees cheerfully announced.

All inside the ring sat rigid and some stood with spears ready.

Tallah and a female gatherer entered the gap in the banana trees. They both had bulky full bags draped over their necks hanging down to their knees.

Nash, Vera, and Koi all exclaimed, "Tallah!" They were visibly excited to see her. Likewise, others rose to greet the gatherer that was with her. Both women quickly stepped backwards so that no one could touch them. It was a rather odd move especially since they both did it at the same time.

"Tallah, what's going on?" Vera asked.
A grin grew across her face. When her mouth could smile no larger, she said in a serious voice,

"We bring weapons." She pointed at the bags the two held. "Some are explosive, so be careful."

After the women had set the bags down very gingerly, they explained. "Once I got to the base camp several women were unpacking some of the things they'd brought with them. They had these large beads in a basket that were being carried with great care. When I asked what it was, they told me about how hunters use these to scare prey out from hiding in the jungle. The beads are a very tiny bit of a natural compound that expands or explodes on impact. It makes a noise and a small flash of light. I sat down with them. They were harmless, just a bit of noise. However, these," she said while pulling a clay ball about the size of a coconut from the bag at her feet.

"These will make a HUGE noise, and a hole in the ground big enough to sit in. They're safe to carry, they can't go off if bumped or dropped slightly, you have to throw them with force, but there's so many in our bags we didn't want to start some chain reaction if you guys rushed in to hug us." The women began passing out what were essentially hooni bombs.

Vera told Tallah about the battle that had ensued that day.

"I passed many dead on my way here. It was disturbing, I can't imagine what it was like to be in the middle in of it." Tallah responded.

She then went on to explain that everyhooni at the base camp now had personal weapons even the children. That most hooni who'd came from the pods brought every knife, and sharp foraging and gardening tool they had. The other bags they'd brought contained extras to be handed out among the Fighting KaiNaandi.

Tallah and the other hooni she'd came with had to leave soon after everyhooni had the weapons they'd brought. They were heading back to the base camp. The parting was bittersweet for everyone. Vera wrapped her arms around Tallah. She didn't want to let go.

"You're brilliant ya know, and I Love you so much. I hope to see you again." Vera told her.

Tallah responded. "I love you too." Then they left.

# CHAPTER TWELVE

Soon everyhooni had settled down to sleep. Within a short while Vera was very aware of a shuffling sound Emanating from the jungle beyond the safety of the banana trees. A few hooni had been trickling in and at first that's all Vera thought the latest sound had been. However now that it got closer the sound was clearly a larger group of hooni. Vera sat very still. She wanted to wake the other KaiNaandi and have them be ready yet this moment like others before it made her remain silent. Hoping that they could stay hidden from the Alpha.

She pointed her spear at the opening and focused on controlling her breathing. Which Bip had stressed when showing them how to throw spears earlier, in what now seemed like a lifetime ago. The wave of hooni were so numerous they all couldn't get through the opening. They were loud enough that Vera didn't have to wake any hooni up, the incoming sound did it for her.

Within seconds the fear unfolded into a joyous reunion. It was a group of hunters who'd been deep in the woods on the extended hunting trip. They'd stopped at the base camp for the night at the foot of the mountain and got the shock of their lives to be told that a war was raging in their absence. They'd also brought with them a group of more than two hundred they'd found wandering in the woods. These other resistant hooni that had heard Eens call and ran to the jungle but didn't know where to go from there were given food and weapons and had everything explained to them as best as it could be.

The most knowledgeable hunters talked about other banana circles like this one spread out through the jungle in surrounding areas nearby. Everyhooni agreed that these would be their best places for sleep and battlefront camps.

Vera asked who would volunteer to head the groups. Each group needs a head count and someone to make decisions. I can't be everywhere; I'm also not qualified at all out here.

She decided to make an announcement before the KaiNaandi broke into groups to head to their own little banana circles.

"Guys, you fought hard today, I'm sorry that L.A.B.S. have turned hooni against hooni, this is horrific to say the least. I again offer anyone who wants to go to the base camp to go at first light. However, know that should the Alpha reach that point, fighting will be inevitable anyway. The bombs Tallah made are a great tool, but I don't want KaiNaandi dying in our attempt to push back the Alpha, so use them sparingly and with great thought.

"I also think we could use their own obedience against them. I say, have a team of two stand visible, one of you yell, 'infected Hooni' the rest of you, lay in wait. They will come to that call, then once you have a lot of Alpha in close enough, ambush them." Vera took a deep breath and continued.

"Also, do not let them reach for your face. One tried to shove the pills into my mouth. If you're genetically susceptible to that you'd be an Alpha and look like a KaiNaandi. We all need to be careful." She paused and looked around. Then added.

"I'm going to need a group of you to go with me to the L.A.B.S. Should I live through tomorrow's battle. I'm going to head there tomorrow night. I believe that only by killing Lorn and Lotta and that family can I stop this. My plan is to destroy the L.A.B.S. and kill the whole line of them. There's no room for that kind of hooni on Dayak."

She stopped and set her gaze on Koi before wrapping up her address to the KaiNaandi.
"That's all I can add. Listen to the Hooni that leads you to your banana circle. They know the jungle and will be your best chance of survival. Goodnight all."

With that she went and grabbed Koi and settled against the farthest point from the opening. She laid down on the warm earth with Koi wrapped around her. The two fell into a deep sleep brought on by physical and mental exhaustion.

Vera opened her eyes to the soft morning light. Beautiful sounds of birds and other jungle animals filled her ears. The faint smell of flowers could be detected on the breeze blowing against her skin. For a brief second it was a wonderful morning. Koi shook her and handed her water. Someone had brought a bucket from the river, and everyone was getting some.

"Eat something" he said sharply. Vera was already looking around and he could see her mind working out plans of what to do. She shoved a handful of nuts and berries into her mouth and washed them down with more water.

She stood up and asked Bip to have scouts sneak towards the main entrance to the hunter gatherer areas and see if any Alpha were gathering.

"Also send word to the other KaiNaandi groups. Tell them to hold their positions. Eat, rest, and wait for the Alpha to make themselves known. When our scouts get back, we'll decide what our next move will be."

She thanked Bip and watched as he told a young thin hunter to go scout.

"Be safe" he warned the scout as he left the banana circle.

Sitting back down on the warm soft earth offered little comfort to Vera. Yesterday she'd started her day as normal, in her house with Tallah. Today it started as the leader of the KaiNaandi army. Looking around at all the faces that were eating and talking amongst themselves she knew their lives were in her hands. That ultimately their death would be her fault.

Her thoughts were soon interrupted. The scout came back in through the opening. His face had the appearance of ash. The color was literally drained from him.

"There's more than I can count! Lines and lines of hooni are forming at the gathering stalls. Lorn is yelling orders at everyhooni!" He told all the hooni who'd gathered around him. Vera quickly sent word to the other members of KaiNaandi.

As quickly as they could the KaiNaandi scrambled into trees and tucked into crevasses between closely growing trees and a few were in holes near fallen logs. They wanted to be able to ambush the Alpha.

Sitting in the crotch of a tree she took her last peaceful breath of the day. The sounds of feet matching in unison could be heard. Lorn could also now be heard yelling. He told the Alpha to enter the jungle and kill all the sick hooni they find.

like dutiful Alpha they left the path and entered the jungle. Vera wondered if the drug that removed their free will also removed their fear. Most of these hooni coming towards them would have never set foot into the jungle before, and now they entered it with the intention to kill.

A few KaiNaandi with bows were stealthily thinning the incoming alpha. Vera could see and hear KaiNaandi jumping onto Alpha from the trees. The screams were filling the air, birds took leave of the area. Even the smallest animals knew this wasn't a safe place today.

Vera saw a large male Alpha come directly under where she sat. She could hear him repeatedly saying Lorns' instructions to himself under his breath. "Kill the sick, kill the sick hooni." It filled her with rage in that instant she knew she wanted to be the hand that killed Lorn.

First though, she'd have to leave the tree. She jumped down directly onto this Alphas back. Plunging her knife into him as the weight of her fall took him to the ground. With a twist of the knife just as Bip had shown them. (It was now he took down hogs and other things he was hunting. He'd said the twist rips open the wound and if it's a lung or heart puncture it will end the animals suffering quickly.) The Alpha didn't even have time to react and was already dead when Vera stood up. Walking away from her first kill of the day she set her sights on finding Lorn.

Up ahead a large group of Alpha were chasing a young KaiNaandi. He ran directly towards Vera yelling for help.

"My weapons are gone!" His only asset was his speed.

He made it to Vera far ahead of the group of five or six Alpha all yelling "infected hooni." And heading their way.

There seemed to be no other KaiNaandi around. Vera pulled out the coconut sized bomb ball and threw it hard at the approaching Alpha. Just as promised it made a huge noise, and flash but, its real power was the explosion. The Alpha were all knocked backwards. All but two lay motionless. The ones that were moving were barely able to crawl.Vera handed the KaiNaandi boy two poofballs and a small deboning knife she had in her waist pouch.

"Come on." She told him as they walked towards the two injured Alpha left after the blast.

When she got to them, they reached for her legs and the boy quickly stabbed one. the other grabbed onto her skirt and pulled her downward.

"Take this medication, you're infected." The Alpha said. Vera shook her head. Even in the terrible physical state of this hooni he was still trying to obey Lorn.

"I'm so sorry." Vera said.

The Alpha grabbed Vera by the knees and in her moment of sympathy the Alpha had been able to overcome her and knocked her to the ground. The Alpha became rough handed and was attempting to get to Vera's face.

Without thinking Vera said, "let me go! Stop it!"

Instantly the Alpha let go and fell still. Vera didn't have a chance to really grasp this because the young KaiNaandi grabbed the Alpha by the head and in a swift motion snapped his neck.

The young KaiNaandi stood panting hard. Tears streaming down his face. Vera stood up and told him thank you. Then told him to find a banana circle and get a new spear.

"This isn't over. You're doing a great job. Now run Hooni." Vera commanded.

He walked a few feet away and popped his poof ball to cover his walk towards a banana circle. Vera resumed her search for Lorn, she was still shocked he was in the jungle. She kept Killing Alpha along the way. Each kill was similar. The Alpha were predictable and didn't hide or try to get away. They were relentless in their pursuit of the KaiNaandi.

Nearing the path Vera saw a KaiNaandi woman being overtaken by three Alpha. They were holding her by the arms and attempting to force the pills into her mouth. There was no way a bomb could helpful, it would kill the KaiNaandi.

Vera just ran full blast at them. Knocking them over and freeing the KaiNaandi. The two women together quickly ended the Alpha. They both were splattered with blood and dirt.

"We're staying together. I'm Pec." She said.

Vera couldn't argue. She now realized that the KaiNaandi should indeed stay in pairs or teams.

"Okay, I'm Vera." She answered. "I'm looking for Lorn. I want to take him out."

Pec laughed. "Obviously I know who you are!" She looked around to make sure no Alpha were coming at them.

"I can see you wanting to take out Lorn. Head off the snake kinda tactic. I saw him earlier. I can't believe he brought himself to the jungle. But I guess it's hard to control the Alpha army from the L.A.B.S. I'll take you back to where I last saw him."

Just like that the two women headed off into the jungle. They walked quickly but were cautious. It was war, the enemy was all around them. Every time they'd make a little progress towards the last place Pec had seen Lorn more Alpha would block the way. Pec was an amazing fighter. She was short and thick, and she used it to her advantage. An alpha ran at her she ducked and rolled into the legs of the charging alpha, knocking him to the ground. As soon as he hit the ground, she made her fatal blow. She had split her spear and wedged her knife in the end. Wrapping it with cordage for extra hold. A simple hard swipe of her spear often cut the throats of the alpha with enormous force.

They came to a clearing where a small stream with a winding path opened the canopy and made a very bright and visible area. Pec and Vera dropped behind a large fallen log.

"He was here." Pec told her.

There were many Alpha in this area. Maybe twenty. Then she saw Lorn. He was sitting on a wooden box. He had one of the clubs like his Alpha soldiers carried in one hand and a sandwich in the other.

"Ya know," Pec talked as softly to Vera as possible. Making it hard to for Vera to hear so she leaned in so close that her ear was almost touching Pec's face.

"The fact that they all carry the same weapon tells me a couple things. One, Lorns' been planning this for awhile and the council meeting the other day wasn't the first time he'd turned a hooni into an Alpha. Someone had to be making all those stupid clubs for him.

"Two, he didn't expect any resistance. Otherwise, he'd have made a weapon that allowed for more self-defense moves. These were just to hit a few disobedient ones of us at close range."

Vera knew Pec was right. Lorn was a planner. He was organized and liked to have total control, obviously. However, he now had the opposite of that. He was probably a bit panicked.

"You're absolutely right." Vera answered.

She sat and watched the Alpha around him. They just stood unless he told them do something.

Vera stated, "I can't attack Lorn with all those Alpha around. They'd stop me and he'd run before I could get to him. I can't throw a bomb, the chances of it landing close enough to kill Lorn are slim, again he'd just get away. I wonder if there are more KaiNaandi around hiding nearby?"

Vera glanced in different directions like a KaiNaandi would just be visible if she looked hard enough.

"There's a banana circle about a five-minute walk from here. We could go gather a few." Pec said with a crooked smile.

They crawled off in the direction of the banana circle. Once they were out of earshot and far enough to not be seen by Lorn they stood. Both women began to run. Pec led the way since she knew where the circle was, but her speed was amazing given her stocky build.

When they got to the banana circle, they found ten or fifteen KaiNaandi inside it. Some were hurt but most just seemed to have stumbled in for water or a sit down. Bip, Nash and Koi were among the Hooni they found in this circle. There was a relief to see each other but no time for celebration. Pec quickly told everyone inside the circle about finding Lorn and that they needed enough KaiNaandi to make it impossible for Lorn to escape so Vera could eliminate him.

"He killed both her mom and dad, he's their leader and she's ours. It's fitting that she be his Executioner."

Vera just listened. Pec was amazing at rallying the KaiNaandi and with what she said, it was obvious that all the KaiNaandi had been talking among themselves about what was going on. Vera's story was becoming legend in the here and now.

Everyhooni agreed. Only one female KaiNaandi chose to stay behind with the injured. They wasted no time and went directly back to the opening where Lorn still sat finishing his lunch.

The KaiNaandi surrounded the alpha. Hidden but close enough to pounce. Two brave KaiNaandi went to the edge farthest from Where Lorn sat and began to yell "infected Hooni!!"

The majority of the Alpha went for it. Running toward that sound. Lorn stood up and watched.

Yelling "kill all non Alpha, I told you that was the new orders stupids!"

# CHAPTER THIRTEEN

The battle between the alpha and KaiNaandi raged outside of the clearing where Lorn could hear but not see what was going on. Nash, Pec, and Koi snuck up behind Lorn with Vera.

In the instant that Nash and Koi grabbed Lorn by both arms and spun him around to face Vera the battle washed its way into the clearing. Like fast rushing flood water. One second nohooni were visible and the next the clearing was covered with them. Lorn yelled for the Alpha to aid him.

Vera wanted to tell him everything that was in her heart. To have this moment of self-fulfilling vindication, but the moment didn't allow it. She plunged her knife into his chest just below the sternum, and with a hard jerking motion pulled it all the way down to his groin.

Everyone gasped. Koi looked down and back at Vera. Lorn looked down as his insides fell from their warm safe body and dangled into the air.

Vera didn't flinch. She simply looked at him, Koi and Nash had let him fall to the ground. They'd had to turn to defend themselves against the Alpha that had now reached where they stood. He gurgled and extended his hand towards Vera. She stepped over him and never looked back. Just jumped into the battle with her fellow KaiNaandi.

It was the largest group fight Vera had been a part of. The Alpha were putting up a hard fight. The KaiNaandi were winning though. More and more Alpha fell and very few KaiNaandi did. The victors now stood in the clearing in a tight huddle. After several tense moments it became clear that no more Alpha were coming at them. They all hugged and cheered. Rejoicing that it was over for the moment.

"Good fight guys!" Bip yelled out.

In an instant that would always confuse Vera, Bip was rushed by three Alpha. They struck him in the back of the head hard. He fell to the ground where the three continued to strike him.

All the KaiNaandi rushed to his side, slaughtering the attacking Alpha. No change in effort would have created a different outcome. Bip had died at the first blow, which cracked his skull. Those clubs were indeed not great, but they were deadly.

Nash and a few other hunters carried his body back to the banana circle. It was a Solemn walk. No one spoke, no Alpha were seen. They sat in the shelter of the banana trees and for the first time felt the gravity of the day.

No one spoke. Nash laid his head on Bips motionless chest and wept. Vera again wished she had words for this moment. Nothing could match the magnitude though. She simply stood next to him and cried too.

It was Pec who broke the sovereignty of the scene. Bursting into the circle from where she'd been standing just outside.

"I am sorry Bip died", she said. "Seems everyhooni's family will be shrunk when this mess is over. But we have to move. I hear Alpha coming this way."

They all had begun to gather their packs and weapons when Vera had an idea.

"Let's see if it's a lot of them and we can just bomb the group. We have to start making numbers matter."

Everyhooni knew Vera was right, so they stayed together and observed the alpha. The pack was about fifteen or so. All repeatedly saying, "kill the sick hooni." With no sign of any hidden KaiNaandi several of their group each threw a bomb hard. Dozens of bombs rained down on the Alpha and when the dust had settled none of them were left standing.

Vera and her little group quickly made their way through the jungle. Picking up other KaiNaandi along the way. Their group had grown massively, and they now actively hunted the Alpha. No more waiting and hiding. The fear they'd had that morning had been replaced with anger and determination.

Within a few hours they couldn't find any more Alpha to take out. They all sat down outside of the largest and main banana circle a couple of campfires were lit and stew pots were quickly put on. The KaiNaandi army had seemingly been victorious that day.

Vera knew it wasn't over. As soon as she ate, she'd begin her trek to the L.A.B.S. to take out Lotta, and her other two children.

She didn't know what she would encounter along the way, but she knew she couldn't go alone. As if by some unspoken bond Koi, Nash and Pec sat down beside her and asked when they were leaving to go stop the madness at its source.

"Nash, you're not going. I won't take no for an answer. You're the most knowledgeable about the jungle and I want you to stay here and tend to things. You've sacrificed enough already. Organize one group to gather and burn the dead. Form another group to take the wounded to the base camp.

"If no Alpha turn up here for twenty-four hours, assume we've won. Take ALL the KaiNaandi to the base camp then. If we can get back to you... we will. If we're not back in a few days at the latest, then you know we died trying."

Vera cleared her throat and continued. "Just take care of Tallah. I don't know what the future holds, but knowing you have her makes me feel somewhat better."

Then she told Koi and Pec that they each need to eat, gather up some weapons and bombs. That they were going to take a half hour nap and go. The two tried to argue over the nap but Vera told them that it was vital. She was unwavering.

"I'm not having us killed because we rushed off like this was a game. We're going to do EVERYTHING to ensure our success."

Walking, once again through the jungle with Pec and Koi she found herself unable to think about what she was going to do once she got to the L.A.B.S., it was almost more than she could wrap her head around, so she stopped trying to formulate a plan. Otherwise, she'd drive herself insane. Instead she focused on being alert for any Alpha. They found a few injured and near death that they mercifully finished. It was visibly difficult for Koi the most. To which at one point he asked the women,

"Neither of you seem rattled to put down our neighbors, and Vera you took Lorn out without hesitation, so violently too."

Pec was first to answer him. "My family raises the pigs that pull carts around Dayak. My mother also liked to collect hurt animals and make them better. Putting something down that needs it, is the ultimate act of love. It's saying, 'I'll do what's best for the other party no matter how hard it is for me.' It's a selfless act. It ends their pain and it's all yours to carry from then on. As far as killing the other Alpha, it's easy when they're going after my throat!"

Vera liked how Pec related ending the suffering of the injured Alpha to a noble deed. In a way ending all the Alpha could be looked at like that, they yell 'infected hooni', yet it's really them that are sick and need help.

She tried to find the best answer for Koi regarding killing Lorn.

"He is evil, he took our parents away, Bip and so many more. All the Alpha We're having to kill are because of him. If I could have tortured him for days on end I would have. He's the only thing I have no guilt over. Defending Dayak feels like what I was created for. I'm scared to lose you Koi, so yes, I'm going to fight for everything to be put right. I'm sorry it bothered you, and rightly so. This is disturbing. It should bother everyhooni. Don't be ashamed of it being unsettling. Use that uneasy feeling to help end this and then teach our future generations to never ignore that uneasy feeling again, so that this never has to be felt by any other hooni."

Koi slid his hand into Veras' and they continued on without speaking. Vera took Pec's hand on the other side and the three walked down the path, past the fish and gathering stalls that stood empty, and onwards towards town and the L.A.B.S. that lay beyond it. Their pace was quick, and they kept their heads on a swivel. Every sound gained attention and every potential threat was sized up.

# CHAPTER FOURTEEN

Their tentative travels went unprovoked. No danger presented itself and they approached the L.A.B.S. building like Dorthey Gale at the gates to the emerald city. Small and meek in appearance but with the power to change everything already inside them.

Vera and Koi talked about finding a way into the building. Climbing to an open window they saw was an option. Sneaking in with a group of Alpha if they shaved their heads and lost their shoes maybe. Pec however had another idea.

She simply walked up to the front door and pushed. It opened, she walked inside and held the door ajar while Vera and Koi sheepishly followed. They said thanks as they passed her.

"It doesn't always have to be difficult; this is Lotta's first war too." Pec said calmly as she let go of the door and they made their way through the empty foyer.

"You're very correct." Vera admitted.

She led the way towards Lotta's office. She knew it well. Being in this building brought back memories of walking hand in hand with her mother when she'd worked here all those years ago. They made it to her office door and gathered around close and low. Vera mouthed the words, 'one, two, three' and flung the door open. Rushing inside the office with weapons at the ready. No one was in it.

Feeling foolish for the second time in such a short span agitated Vera. Koi picked up an object from the desktop and threw it hard against the wall. His feelings finally bubbling over.

"She'll be in the east hall." Without anything more, he walked out leading the way. Both women followed without question.

Once they neared the east hall it was clear Koi was right. Hooni could be heard walking around. Lotta's voice could also be heard as She barked orders. Koi led them up a stairway that went to a gallery above the large room where Lotta was. This room was used for lectures and demonstrations among the scientists. The three laid down on their bellies to observe.

The Alpha were broken into several groups. Some were cooking, others were making club weapons. They weren't sure what some of the groups were doing, but nonetheless Lotta walked around scolding and smacking the Alpha under her control.

"When Lorn returns you will be taken to the jungle to fight the sick Hooni! Hurry up with those clubs." Lotta spat as she went by the group of hooni hurriedly working on the clubs.

The room was full of alpha. Throwing multiple bombs as fast as they could seemed like the only clear way to handle this. They'd have to wait until Lotta was directly under them to do it. They couldn't leave anything up to chance and risk her getting away to fight another day.

Just as Vera was about to tell her plan to the other two, she felt a tapping at her ankle. At first, she dismissed it as maybe Koi or Pec tapping at her with their foot absent mindedly, but then she could clearly tell it was a finger and not a bump from anyhooni's careless foot.

Her eyes grew wide, and she was nearly frozen with fear. She needed to turn around, but she couldn't. She managed to glance at Koi and Pec. When the sideways glances from their fear idled faces looked back at her she knew they too were being tapped.

Slowly they turned their heads to see who was tapping at them. To their horror it was Lotta's oldest daughter, Nefthra. She was about a year or so younger than Lorn, and a couple years older than Phi, the bossy baby of Lotta's kids.

Nefthra placed her finger over her lips in the typical 'shh' position.

Vera clenched her jaw and rolled her eyes. They had no choice but to obey Nefthra, if they tried to fight back, they'd be heard by the room full of Alpha below. Slowly they followed her away from the balcony and out into the hallway. When they reached the hallway Vera lunged forward pinning Nefthra to the wall.

"You're really gonna want to NOT kill me." She said softly.

Pec clapped back in a harsh tone, "oh yeah, why's that?"

Nefthra hung her head before answering, "I can make sure you get to my mother and sister without any Alpha around."

The three didn't really know what to say. They just exchanged confused glances.

"I don't agree with what they're doing, and I want to help you stop it." She added.

Vera let her go and asked, "you realize I'm here to kill them, don't you?"

Nefthra shook her head and avoided eye contact. "I've thought about killing them for years. They're horrible hooni. I can't sit by and do nothing through this. I also can't force my hand to kill them. If I had done it years ago none of this would be happening."

Believing her sent up red flags in Vera's mind but they really didn't have much to lose.

"Okay, what's your plan?" Vera asked.

Koi and Pec shifted their weight from one foot to the other visibly uncomfortable, but they said nothing. This conversation and assessment of her honesty was clearly beyond their scope and Vera was better able to understand the complexities of what Nefthra was proposing.

"They eat dinner together, every day in a little den mother had made a few years ago. No Alpha will be there. They will eat alone; I'm supposed to be there. I'm generally late. The door is unlocked, and they'd be expecting me to walk in. You'd have both the element of surprise and the benefit of them being alone, seated and unprepared." Nefthra said finally looking up to meet Vera's face.

It was obvious that this pained her to tell, but her need to be on the right side of this was also obvious. Vera agreed and the three were led away by Nefthra, down a long hallway. At the end of the hall, it made a right turn to a dead end.

"This is a supply closet." Nefthra informed them. Patting the door at the dead end. "This is where you can hide and wait. The den is two doors up on the right." She said pointing back in the direction they'd just came.

"How do we know you're not standing us here to be slaughtered?" Koi asked.

"Because I'm standing here with you. I'm not going anywhere. They will be along in under ten minutes to eat. Mother is very punctual and the whole family can be strict about following guidelines with that said, Phi is dutiful and will definitely be with her."

They opened the closet and stepped inside. Brooms and dusters hung on the wall. The faint smell of a damp mop filled the air with a hint of the mundane, which was in direct opposition of the actual moment at hand.

Wooden crates were scattered about in the closet and they each took a seat on one.

"Your moms were always so nice to me." Nefthra said, breaking the awkward silence. "They talked to me all the time. Treated me so warmly. I had just started working here the morning I found them dead. I will see that image in my memory forever. The two of them, just sitting in their chairs with their head on the desk. Almost like they'd fell asleep working. I know now mother did that, I'm so sorry" She looked from Vera to Koi.

Before anyone could say another word sounds of heavy steps and a rolling cart could be heard in the hallway.

Phi could be heard saying, "Mother what are we eating?"

Lotta responded with, "whatever the Alpha cooked us. The hunter gatherer stands are down, and our food is limited. Don't worry darling, we'll have the painted idiots back in line soon and then we can have all your favorite foods again."

The conversation ended as they reached the door to their den. It's opening and closing caused the door to the supply closet to jiggle a bit.

"Let's give them enough time to get sat down and eating." Vera whispered to her little band of KaiNaandi, who'd now grown by one.

"Nefthra stay here. We'll come back for you afterwards." She began to protest to which Vera simply said, "No, this isn't something that should be in your head forever Nefthra."

She sat back down and accepted what Vera had said. The three opened and closed the supply closet door with care. Hoping to make no sound. They readied their knives and crept up to the door holding their weapons. Their hearts all beating so hard it pounded in their ears.

Images of her mom, dad, and Bip flashed in her mind. 'They didn't deserve to die, but Lotta and Phi do' she told herself. She then thought about Tallah, and all the kids sitting at the base camp. They deserved a good safe life, free from the fear of becoming an Alpha or a science experiment.

She flung open the door bringing all the KaiNaandi and her hope of freedom along with her. Phi was seated nearest to the door and Pec stabbed her with the knife she had on the end of her spear. Lotta stood and screamed for her daughter who lay bleeding and twitching on the floor.

In a shocking turn of events Koi jumped onto the table and ran at Lotta. Kicking her in the face as she started to stand up. This knocked her backwards into her seat and away from the table about a foot and half. With a surge of adrenaline that had come out of nowhere he grabbed her hands and quickly pulled them behind the chair. Binding them with twine he'd had in his waist bag.

Pec had slit Phi's throat by this point and now went and casually took a chair to the door, sat it against it and settled herself into it as if she was somewhere between guarding the door and watching a show.

Vera stood staring at Lotta. She pulled from her pocket a handful of pills she'd taken off one of the Alpha.

"Open your mouth and take your medicine, you sick hooni!" Vera said, almost in an unrecognizable voice.

Lotta refused to comply, pressing her lips firmly together. Vera leaned over and again said, "take the pills!"

When she refused this time, she spit in Vera's face. Vera took her knife and sliced Lotta's arm. "Take the pills." She demanded and sliced Lotta again. The pain forced Lotta into submission. She opened her mouth and swallowed the pills.

Within minutes Lotta's body went slack and she clearly gave into the submissive role of an Alpha. To which Vera had planned all along her walk towards the L.A.B.S..

"Where are your stockpiles of this Alpha drug?" She asked.

"In the upper halls, in boxes." was her answer.

"Has it already been put into the water supply for the town?" Vera demanded.

"No, we haven't figured out how to get into the water tanks yet." She said in a frustrated tone."

"Is there an antidote to reverse the Alpha?" She asked lastly.

Lotta's laughter let her know that while she may be an Alpha, some resistance was inside Lotta. As she laughed, she shook her head no.

"In the name of the KaiNaandi, may your death put an end to your selfish plans." Vera raised her knife. Before she struck Lotta began to beg.

"I'll put you in charge, you can help run my new world. You'd never have to work or want for anything. You'd have a big house, all the food you want. Servants!! You'd be able to rule the world by my side!" Lotta said tearfully.

She was obviously fighting against the Alpha drugs and in her effort to keep control and save her life she was showing the greed and madness inside.

"We can continue to work on my super drugs, we can turn ourselves into a new race. We're clearly smarter than most of these hooni anyway, now we can be prettier, faster, larger. You know you and I are different; My DNA makes these mind control drugs short lived in my system. You and Lorn could be married and start making the heirs to my throne. We're destined to be in power Vera, untie me. We ARE the Alpha Join me!"

Vera had felt different inside from all the other hooni her whole life. She never felt like she belonged. Standing here looking at Lotta offering the world was indeed tempting. Koi and Pec nervously watched Vera answer her.

"I am already greater than you Lotta. You're a disease on this island! Your body will burn just like the ones you deem inferior. Your name will be erased from history and your memory will be a cautionary tale to anyhooni that may one day think they should be above the rest." She put her blade to Lotta's throat. "Oh, and I already killed Lorn. Your line is extinct."

With that Vera sliced Lotta's neck from ear to ear. As the blood flowed out Lotta went still. Vera dipped her hand into the sticky red blood and made a swipe across her own upper arm. Three lines of red blood. She then did the same to Koi, and Pec. No one spoke. The silent ceremony didn't need words. They all understood that it meant this blood was spilled with purpose. To never forget.

They ran back to the supply closet and found Nefthra anxiously waiting for them. She knew by the blood that her mother and sister were gone.

"We have to Destroy the boxes of Alpha drug." Vera said as she led the way.

"I don't know where mother kept it." Nefthra replied.

"We do." Koi told her.

Pounding up the stairs together they passed an Alpha. Koi killed him quickly and they continued on their way. Once they reached the hallway that the drugs were being hidden in the Alpha guarding it came at them in full force. Pec handed Nefthra a knife and the four sliced and slammed their way towards the boxes. Vera threw a bomb into the crowd of Alpha but inside it didn't have the same action. It was so loud it sent everyhooni's ears ringing. It killed a few Alpha but did little damage otherwise.

Several Alpha were on top of them. Nefthra was dead quickly. Pec and Koi were being held down by Alpha and were fighting with everything they had. Vera was still standing and swinging her spear wildly to try and get to Koi and Pec. It was useless. They were too outnumbered.

"STOP Fighting!" She yelled with all the tenacity she had. To her disbelief all the Alpha froze.

Vera yelled. "Line up on the wall!"

Again, all the Alpha went and lined up.

"Vera, they obey any true Alpha." Koi stammered. "Alpha, like a dominant personality!

Lorn and Lotta must have named them Alpha army because of that. They aren't The Alpha they are Alpha's army. Holy cow, they are the army FOR the Alpha. Remember our moms wrote in the letter that the medication we'd been given all our lives removed the Alpha ability to be dominant. or controlling... you have that ability."

Pec added, "Like an Alpha monkey... the Beta monkeys obey."

That was what the drug did. It made sense to Vera now. It controlled them because it removed their ability to disobey the Alpha. Their own common sense was suspended.

She wanted to slide to the floor and crumple into a ball. She knew now that it was all over. She could save any hooni who were Alpha.

"Go gather ALL the alpha and line everyhooni up in front of the building." She ordered the Alpha's army.

Vera, Koi, and Pec walked outside. They were dirty and tired. They hugged and held each other. Amazed that this whole thing was over for the most part. When all the Alpha stood in lines she instructed them to burn the L.A.B.S. building. They dutifully did as she told them.

Over the next day Vera marched the Alpha through every Pod on Dayak. Rounding up anyhooni who had remained in their homes.

When they made it to the edge of the jungle, she stood the Alpha under the roofs of the gathering stalls and told them to sit and not move. Koi and Pec handed out water and Vera went off in search of Bip and Tallah.

# CHAPTER FIFTEEN

It took her two hours to reach the base camp at the mountain. She gave them all the abridged version of what happened with promises to retell it in full. Een brought his machine that allowed Vera's voice to be amplified. It was then that she told everyhooni everything. From what had happened to her and Koi's parents. To the lock box with the letter. To how the original Omega team had changed the biochemistry of everyhooni's brains which in turn is the real reason they aren't human anymore.

How Lotta and Lorn thought they'd create a new super race and divide the island, making most of them slaves. She told them that the whole family were dead. That Nefthra had aided them and died trying to ensure everyhooni's freedom.

"Proof that we aren't just the product of our DNA." She added.

Then went onto explain that the Alpha's army were no longer a threat. That their participation in the war was not their fault.

"Do NOT hold what happened against them, we'll only sow seeds of hate that will grow into the next war." She warned.

"There is no, us and them. From now on, all Hooni are one KaiNaandi!"

Tallah came and stood next to Vera while she spoke. Koi was at her other side. She could see other familiar faces making their way to the front of the crowd.

"The L.A.B.S. are gone. We burned them. No longer will we give our babies the injections. We will have autonomy over ourselves. I will put together a new council to ensure that life on Dayak remain harmonious. Let us truly become what the Omega wanted. A peaceful Island filled with happiness and joy."

She looked at the Alpha's army. Their heads shaved and their feet bloody from walking barefooted. She was filled with pity for them. She wasn't sure how to handle them either. So instead of trying to find the right way to fix it she just spoke from her heart.

"Alpha, listen! You have been used as a weapon by a corrupt family in attempt for power. This wasn't your fault. You will carry no guilt for it, but you also won't forget it." As Vera was giving her orders to the Alpha, she knew she didn't want to control them, nor allow for anyone else to be able to control them ever again.

"You will never blindly follow orders again. You know right from wrong and from here on out will use the scales of justice within yourself. From now on, you will choose your own actions and never again will you harm anyone. I need you to snap out of this trance you're in."

The Alpha blinked a few times and looked around. The KaiNaandi welcomed them, and shared food and they all tended to each other's wounds. As she began to walk away from the microphone, she remembered one more thing.

"Oh yeah, today is Hooni day. How fitting." She said in a flat way.

Lady Vazeet took the microphone and began to talk to the crowd about how they could move forward after such an unspeakable tragedy. Tallah hugged Vera. They held one another tightly.

"I was worried I'd never see you again" Tallah cried.

The two women held each other as Bip, and Koi stood beside them.

"Let's end this horrific day with something worthy of celebrating shall we!" Lady Vazeet said in a lively and upbeat voice. Which got everyhooni's attention. She opened her hands and invited the two couples to come forward.

"Are you ready to be joined so that you're coupled forever from this day on?" Vazeet asked both women.

Tallah and Vera looked at Bip and Koi. A smile and a nod from them were all they needed. Vazeet announced over the speaker. "A double wedding it is for this first KaiNaandi Hooni day!"

She married them before all Of Dayak. Weddings were not an elaborate event, but it was always a joyous time. It somehow helped to remove the sting of all that was lost over the short war. It was an act of unity among a group of hooni who'd just earlier that day seemed destined to be divided. What was to be a violent future now seemed promising.

When the world was at its darkest, the clouds parted, and the sun shown. Disaster was averted and the KaiNaandi continued to change and grow into a new race governed by love and happiness. Common sense and genuine concern for their neighbors harkened in a new era.

Generations upon generations told of how greed and entitlement almost led to their downfall. It was never forgotten.

---

Hooni were a long-gone memory of the KaiNaandi's evolutionary past. They filled history books and lended themselves to children's stories. Every KaiNaandi gave a lot of attention to the archaic people, because their near demise shaped the KaiNaandi's civilization.

The KaiNaandi had finally achieved harmony. Their population had grown too large to stay on the island called Dayak that had been their home for all recorded history.

A council meeting was taking place that day to select the members that would leave the island and explore the world beyond to prepare for a migration across the planet.

Zeentee sat quietly sipping her coffee hoping she would be selected to go. She yearned for adventure. That however is a tale for another book.


## The End


*Next in the series is Zee tee's Generation.*